OTTERS IN SPACE 4

FIRST MOUSTRONAUT

MARY E. LOWD

This book is dedicated to everyone who has fought for and continues to fight for reproductive justice. Abortion is a fundamental part of healthcare and a basic human right.

CONTENTS

CHAPTER 1
YVETTE

The mouse whirled through the air, paws hitting the gym mat in rhythm as she flipped: front paws, back paws, front paws. Head over tail. Her long tail streamed behind her, making fancy curlicues in the wake of her carefully practiced routine. Finally, Yvette pirouetted up to the high bar, spun around it and launched even higher into the air—nearly flying.

When she came down, the mouse landed—perfectly—in the center of the mat, all four paws on the ground. She drew a deep breath, and then rose up, standing just long enough to smile at the crowd, before taking her bow.

Yvette always felt a little lost, almost dizzy, in the moments after she finished a routine in front of a crowd. While she was flipping, she knew exactly what to do. The movements were measured, precise, practiced. Afterwards, her hind paws betrayed her, stumbling, as the weight of the audience's expectations fell on her shoulders. The roar of their applause crashed over her like a wave, and she tried to enjoy the moment. The dizzy, overwhelming moment. She bowed again, trying not to worry yet about her score.

Yvette had never won first place at a competition—second

sometimes, third often. Never first. And she didn't want to jinx her chances by caring... too much. Or at all. She scurried off the mat, dusting the white chalk off her paws that made the bars easier to grip. It left smears on her bright red leotard, and her gray fur would be full of it later; it always was. Practice every day; get your fur full of chalk every day.

When Yvette reached the sidelines, her mother and then her trainer hugged her, each in turn.

"You did great," her mother said.

Her trainer nodded, meaning Yvette had done well. But then she started twisting up her tail in knots, meaning maybe Yvette hadn't done well enough.

Yvette turned away from the scoreboard where the judges' scores would soon appear in harsh red lights. She looked at the crowd of mice in the bleachers instead. They looked happy, excited. They'd watched her perform, and her performance had made them happy. Maybe that was enough. That was why she did this—not the score.

At the far side of the bleachers filled with mice, crouching down to fit inside the auditorium, were two unusual members of the crowd—a gray striped tabby cat and a river otter with green zebra stripes dyed into his brown fur, both of them wearing navy-blue uniforms. They were giants compared to everyone else. Yvette couldn't possibly have missed them in the crowd before. They must have come in during her performance.

What were a cat and otter doing in Mousfordshire? And even more bizarrely, watching a gymnastics meet?

The murmuring in the crowd turned sour, and Yvette lost interest in the strange visitors. She knew what the change in the crowd's voices meant. Instead of looking up at the scoreboard, she turned to her mother, and her mother simply shook her head.

Yvette nodded. She hadn't expected to win. She didn't mind.

Really. Except, her stomach felt like it had fallen inside of itself. She had to keep smiling, whiskers turned up, for the audience. Brave and graceful. Always graceful, whether flipping through the air—which she enjoyed—or facing dismal scores. Which she did not.

Yvette didn't like losing, but then who did?

"Next time," her trainer said with a falsely cheerful smile. The smile didn't reach all the way to her whiskers.

"Let's get out of here," her mother said.

Yvette nodded, relieved at the idea. She didn't want to stay around and watch the rest of the performances. "I could use a basket of greasy corn fries and a very cold blackberry juice." As cold as her heart felt.

"Go get ready, and I'll meet you outside."

"I'll see you at practice on Monday?" her trainer asked.

Yvette nodded, but she wasn't sure. She couldn't face the idea of a 'next time' right now. Or maybe at all. Eventually, it would be time to give gymnastics up and get serious about using her moldering engineering degree. Design some bridges or high-rise buildings. Something real and solid that would last, instead of dissipating into so many videos on the internet—ephemeral moments that passed into memories as fast as the enormous clock Mousfordshire was built around could tick off the seconds in a day.

Yvette made her way to the locker rooms, changed out of her leotard into street clothes, and then disappeared into the crowds on her way out. Just another mouse. No longer an athlete. Anonymous. Or so she thought, until a very large foot stepped in front of her on the street outside.

A cat's paw.

Otters weren't an unusual sight around Mousfordshire. If one day, Yvette designed a building that actually got built, a team of otters would likely do most of the actual construction. They were giants among mice. Hiring a couple otters to come into town and construct a building was simply more efficient than having the mice who lived there do it.

Cats on the other hand were rare, most of them lived across the pond in the Uplifted States. Yvette had never seen one in person before. And now one was standing, pointedly, in her way.

"What do you want?" Yvette squeaked up at the cat who was easily more than four times her height. "Don't most of you cats stick to the Uplifted States? So, what're you doing here, blocking my way?"

The cat's face, staring down at her, made Yvette's skin crawl and her fur ruffle. Those feline eyes, green and glinting, looked at the mouse too possessively. And her teeth looked very large and sharp. Yvette shuffled her hind paws in a restless, nervous dance. She'd never felt so aware of her own size before, and she didn't like it.

The cat said in a purring voice, "My name is Kipper Brighton, and I have a proposition for you."

"Wait..." Suddenly, Yvette recognized the tabby cat. She'd seen her after all. This tabby was all over the news last year. "You're that space cat. The hero of Europa."

"That's right," Kipper purred. "I'm in charge of the new Uplifted States space program. And we're looking for mouse recruits."

Other mice scurried along the streets, walking around the giant cat who was too large to enter most of the buildings around her. Plenty of other mice. "Why me?" Yvette asked. "You want a gymnast with a side degree in engineering?" She almost laughed, but the cat replied:

"Yes, that's exactly what I want."

Yvette noticed the otter who'd been with Kipper before, the one with brightly dyed fur, just around the corner of the sports complex building. His long spine was bent forward, so he could lean down. He was talking to a mouse—oh, he had found Yvette's mother. That was good, she supposed. If Kipper's otter associate was talking to her, then at least Yvette's mother wasn't worried about why she was taking so long.

"I have a life and commitments here," Yvette said. "I imagine your space program would involve moving to the Uplifted States." Nothing Yvette had ever heard about the Uplifted States had made it sound like a good place for a mouse. From what she'd heard, in fact, it wasn't even a great place for cats. Dogs ruled the roost there.

"At first, yes," Kipper admitted. The way her eyes flitted away, not even looking at Yvette as she said 'yes' suggested she knew exactly how unpleasant life in the Uplifted States could be. "But in a matter of months, we expect to begin trial flights. So, actually, it would involve moving to... space."

Yvette knew there were some nice mouse villages on the various otter space stations. Even so, this whole conversation felt like a dream. Minutes ago, she'd been performing a routine that she'd been practicing for months. Every move memorized. Right down to the sad but *graceful* smile she'd rehearsed for when she didn't win.

Now everything was off the rails. No script here to lean on. She didn't know what to say at all. And yet...

Yvette found herself remembering a year ago, when she'd placed third at the same competition. A respectable placement. The honor had even come with a shiny, bronze medallion on a bright, red ribbon. She'd hung it on her wall with the one from the year before, and the year before that, all won while she'd still been finishing her engineering degree. Then she'd spent two days in bed, feeling bad about herself. Even worse because —she told herself—she had no right to feel sad in the first place. She'd placed third. She should be grateful to have done so well. Most gymnasts didn't win a medal at all.

No, wait... That had been two years ago. Last year, she'd

shaped up and done better. The third-place medal had rolled off her like water on an otter.

Although, she recalled that she had still spent two days in bed moping. She'd simply blamed it on her model bridge breaking. The model had been her thesis project, and she had genuinely put many hours of work into it. Still...

The days she'd spent in bed moping correlated awfully closely with the days that she'd competed and her grasp had fallen just short of her dream.

Yvette didn't want to waste two days moping. And she didn't want to get back to practicing with her trainer. Maybe a trip to space was exactly what she needed. An escape. An entirely new life. "Okay, I'm curious. Is there somewhere we can go, so you can tell me more about it?"

None of the restaurants Yvette was familiar with catered to... giants. She supposed there might be a cafe somewhere with outdoor seating, but when she glanced up to check, the sky was gray. Classic, drizzly New London weather all around the Big Ben clocktower.

All of the mouse buildings that had been constructed inside the ruins of the Palace of Westminster, attached to Big Ben, would be too small for Kipper and her otter friend. Still, there had to be somewhere out here that catered to the otters who came into town to do work. Although, she supposed, otters might not mind eating in the rain as much as mice did. Or probably cats.

"Look, I've never been to Mousfordshire before," Kipper said. "But my associate, Trugger—" She gestured with a gray paw at the green-striped otter. "He has been."

"Alright," Yvette said, stepping away from the cat and heading towards her mother and the otter.

Trugger was every bit as large as Kipper, but somehow, his lively presence felt less threatening. He seemed more likely to cause damage accidentally—say by stepping carelessly and swinging his rudder tail into a building—than to psychopathically snap and start eating mice.

Yvette knew that uplifted cats didn't eat uplifted mice. Maybe she'd just seen too many nature videos about the feral animals that still existed in the world—lions, cheetahs, tigers. Big cats. And to Yvette, Kipper really did look big. She wouldn't actually fit inside the cat's mouth in one bite... but close.

"Hey, Trugger," Kipper said. She was still standing half a block away from him. A mouse-sized block. For a cat and otter, that seemed to be a comfortable, conversational distance. "What was that restaurant you wanted to go to?"

"Fish-Man Jack's!" Trugger exclaimed, clapping his paws and hopping dangerously up and down. All of the mice near him scurried to a safer distance.

"Wait," Yvette squeaked, loudly to make sure the otter could hear her. "Didn't that place close down a couple years ago?" And from what she could remember, it was an otter-run joint on the fringe of Mousfordshire, at least half an hour's walk away. And it wasn't like Trugger and Kipper would fit in a cab with Yvette and her mother...

"It's also a little far from here," Yvette's mother said, looking worried. Her thinking had clearly run parallel to Yvette's.

"Oh, don't worry about that, Vonda," Trugger said, chummily, as if he'd been best friends with Yvette's mother for years. "You can ride on my shoulder and keep telling me about all the different fancy leotards you sewed for Yvie's competitions when she was little. Well... even littler!"

Vonda chortled, and Yvette realized that this otter—who might soon be her colleague, if she took this new job offer—was going to know all about her ninja, princess, and space warrior phases as a child. Her mother loved talking about those costumes.

Also, why did she already have a nickname? Even her mother didn't call her "Yvie."

Yvette looked up at Kipper and caught a gleam of sympathy in the tabby cat's eye. "He'll drop the nickname if you ask," Kipper said. "He used to call me Kipster." Her ears skewed, and her eyes rolled. "Look, if you're okay with it, I can give you a ride too."

Vonda was already sitting happily on Trugger's shoulder, so Yvette shrugged. She might as well ride on a cat's shoulder to a closed down otter restaurant. This was turning out to be the strangest day.

Kipper knelt down, and Yvette climbed onto her shoulder. She clung tightly to the collar of the cat's uniform. At first she was nervous, watching the city glide by from such an awkward in-between height—high enough to hurt if she fell, but still lower than the roofs of the multi-story buildings they passed by. But as she settled into the rhythm of the cat's pace, she began to see how convenient it might be to be a giant.

When they got to the edge of Mousfordshire, there was no wall or sign. Nothing that explicitly demarked the difference between the mouse town and the otter outskirts. But the change was obvious. Buildings were five times as tall; the streets widened drastically. When Yvette was younger—a college mouse—she'd loved venturing out to the outskirts with her friends late at night. Avoiding studying. Escaping the pressure of exams. It had felt adventurous. And there were more than a few otter restaurants that catered specifically to adventure-seeking college mice like she'd been.

That's how she knew Fish-Man Jack's had closed down. A group of her college buddies, after graduation, had tried to go there. But the greasy diner was no more.

Sure enough, when they arrived at the building with blue fish painted all over its walls and a roof shaped like a spouting whale, Fish-Man Jack's was gone. Closed down two years ago, just like Yvette had thought. But the restaurant that had taken its place had a really boring name: Sushi Central. So, Yvette could kind of sympathize with Trugger stubbornly continuing to call it Fish-Man Jack's. She might do the same.

Sushi Central was quiet inside, except for a few otter regulars. Kipper and Trugger were invited to take stools at a counter with an elevated conveyer belt that ran down the middle. Sushi morsels on fish-shaped plates streamed by on the conveyer. A sea otter wearing an apron—also decorated with fish—brought over a tiny table and pair of chairs. Well, they looked tiny in his paws, but usually Yvette would think of them as normal-sized. He set them up on top of the counter, so Yvette and Vonda could sit comfortably beside Kipper and Trugger.

The apron-clad otter daintily unfolded a cloth napkin and laid it over Yvette and Vonda's tiny table. A perfect table cloth for them.

"Would you like to order anything?" he asked.

Yvette glanced nervously at the sushi streaming by. Slabs of raw fish, glistening pink and yellow on giant balls of sticky rice, didn't strike her as a particularly appealing meal. But she didn't know what else a place like this offered.

"We're good," Trugger said, dismissing the waiter. Once he was gone, the river otter busied himself grabbing table-sized fish-shaped plates from the conveyer. "If I may, I'd like to suggest a few things." He unwrapped a pair of spear-sized chopsticks and stabbed a spherical confection right through the middle. "This is a sesame ball with red bean paste inside." He waved it around on his chopstick. Yvette marveled at the fact that it didn't go flying off.

Vonda was less skeptical, less worried, and apparently much more in the mood for a random adventure with an unpredictable otter leading their way. "Looks lovely!" she declared.

"Excellent." Trugger pulled a sword-sized pocket knife out of one of the pockets in his uniform and sliced off an edge of the sesame ball. The golden, sesame-encrusted pastry was indeed filled with a red paste. He placed it inside a small, flat bowl, probably meant for dipping condiments, and then carefully placed the bowl on their little table. It made a perfect platter.

Next Trugger supplied them with a condiment bowl's worth of seaweed salad and another one filled with sticky rice topped with mango. Each entree he served them came apportioned from the much larger versions he kept for himself.

While Trugger served the mice, Kipper kept her gleaming eyes focused on the conveyer, and every time a pink slip of salmon sashimi or nigiri came gliding by, she reached out with snatching paws. The civilized, uplifted version of a cat pouncing on prey.

Yvette had never really been a mouse who dreamed of leaving her world. Sure, she'd had a space warrior phase as a pup, but who hadn't? Her mother had made a shiny, silver spandex leotard for her, and she'd worn a plastic bubble helmet that had thrown off her balance during flips.

But her dreams of space back then had been filled with other mice. The vast, unmeasurable reaches of space... on her scale. Mice battling mice with glowing laser swords. Mice flying mouse-sized spaceships.

Actual outer space had been mostly populated by otters, since humanity disappeared from Earth during the Dark Times. And she'd never dreamed about living somewhere that the doors were too large to open and the tabletops too high to reach. She didn't want to live among giants, in a world built for them.

That sounded more like a nightmare than a dream.

"Okay," she said. "Let's cut to the..." Yvette stumbled over her own choice of words as she was struck with a far too literal visualization of them. "...um, *chase*. Why me? Why a mouse?"

Kipper ate several of the glistening slabs of salmon, leaving the balls of sticky rice from the pieces of nigiri behind. Trugger sniped them from her plate, squished them together into a giant ball of rice, and stuffed his muzzle full, as if someone had dared him to fit as much rice in his mouth as he could. But no one had.

Kipper stared at the conveyer for a while, her eyes following each plate with salmon like she might pounce again. Instead, she sighed deeply and said, "There's a limit to what I can tell you, legally, before you sign on to the project. I assume you followed the news about the ancient octopus base recovered on Europa?"

A safe bet, since that was how Yvette recognized Kipper. Still, the mouse nodded in confirmation.

Kipper continued: "What I can say is that... schematics... for some very... powerful... technologies were recovered from that base. And we're working to implement those technologies as fast as we can, and also to adapt them for use by, well, a non-octopus crew."

"Although, we do have two octopuses in our crew!" Trugger interjected, cheerfully, still chewing on his giant wad of sticky rice.

Kipper's ears flattened. "Technically, we have one octopus who we've reached out to but hasn't agreed to join the crew yet, and another who would like to... but has been struggling against the more bureaucratic parts of the Uplifted States government to get the necessary clearances."

"Right," Trugger agreed. "Two."

"Are any other mice signed on?" Vonda addressed the question to Trugger. Yvette's mother seemed kind of smitten with the cheerful, zany giant.

"Uh, not yet," Kipper admitted, reluctantly.

Trugger announced, perhaps a little too forthrightly: "The consensus from the engineers and tech experts we've approached so far seems to be that our mission goals are a fool's errand and that only a mouse who was a fool would sign on to a project run by a cat and otter within a dog majority society. So, fools all around. But being foolish is fun, and you should show them all who the real fool is!"

"Me?" Yvette asked.

"Exactly!" Trugger agreed. "At least, that's what we're hoping." He winked at her, as if they were in on the same joke, instead of him just agreeing that she'd be a fool to join their project.

Kipper shook her head. "Our goals are... ambitious, but whether we achieve them or not is secondary to the progress that can be made by striving for them."

"What are your goals?" Yvette picked at the sticky rice in front of her. The slightly sweet and sour taste was very pleasant. "Space exploration? Founding new space stations for the Uplifted States?" There were quite a few otter space stations in the solar system already, but dogs and cats had mostly kept their paws on Earth. Like mice.

Kipper and Trugger exchanged a glance that said they knew their next words were going to sound silly, and they each wanted the other one to actually say them. Finally Kipper folded and said, "We're going to find the missing humans."

"Humans," Yvette repeated. Her mother just laughed. "They died out... ages ago. During the Dark Times, from a plague. I mean, everyone knows that. Except, I guess, for some fringe dog religions..."

Kipper's slanted ears and down-turned whiskers spoke volumes.

"Oh, right, it's not a fringe religion in the Uplifted States." Yvette suddenly felt self-conscious and awkward. Was she dealing with true believers here? She'd never met anyone who thought of humans as gods instead of merely another species on Earth who had, thankfully, managed to uplift several other species before dying out in the great plague. "I'm sorry—I didn't mean to make fun of your beliefs."

Kipper snorted. "I'm not a First Racer. But there is archeological evidence to support, at least, one specific aspect of First Racer beliefs: humans left the Earth before the Dark Times. And for all we know, they may still be out there."

"So what?" Yvette asked.

At almost the same time, her mother blurted out, "Who cares! It's not like they're gods, no matter what some star-struck dogs think."

"We don't think they're gods," Trugger said. "But we do think that if they evolved on Earth before us, made it to the stars before us, and are still living out there—maybe they have some knowledge worth learning."

"Have they terraformed new worlds?" Kipper asked. "Developed better technologies? Isn't that worth knowing?"

Yvette didn't know what to say. The cat and otter made some reasonable points. But she wasn't sure that the mice they'd approached before her were wrong—this did sound like a fool's errand.

"I suppose you're financing the trip by telling a bunch of dogs that they'll get to meet their gods?" Vonda asked drily.

Kipper shrugged. "I'm not in charge of what any dogs think. All I can do is relay the facts. If they want to believe that our space mission will bring them face to face with their gods... well, I suppose it does help pay the bills."

Vonda laughed again. "Oh, you giants with your heads in the sky are always so silly."

Yvette tilted her head and looked at her mother, trying to read what she really thought about the situation. Sure, it was fun, as a joke, to eat sticky rice and mango with giants, while they told you silly stories about their plans to adventure through the stars. But... How would her mother take it if Yvette really went with them? "This still doesn't explain why you need mice. Or, more particularly, a gymnast mouse."

"The octopus technology that we've been adapting," Kipper

said, "is designed for people who can... squeeze through very small spaces."

"Octopi are basically liquid," Trugger said, helpfully but completely inaccurately.

"We've been able to scale up the empty spaces, the access spaces, around the engines we're building... but not enough for cats or otters—"

"Or small dogs!" Trugger interjected. "Or even squirrels!"

"—to fit comfortably inside them for maintenance purposes. We need crew members who are... small and agile."

"Gymnast mice," Yvette said.

"Exactly." Trugger popped another extra giant sushi, composed of several normally giant sushi rolls smooshed together, into his mouth.

"However, since they'll be maintaining a—" Kipper cut herself off, seemingly stopping herself from revealing confidential information. "—a highly technical engine, we need crew mice with proven, tested technical abilities."

"Thus me," Yvette said. "I sit at the cross-section of gymnastics and engineering. How did you find me?"

"We checked the names of all of the mice who'd placed in gymnastics meets in the last year, looking for any who also held degrees in engineering," Trugger said. "And that led us to you. Just you."

Silver and bronze medals might not have been the gleaming gold Yvette dreamed about, but they'd been glittery enough to catch the eye of giants. That was something. Quite something.

"We were actually hoping," Kipper added, "that you could recommend some other mice who would be good for and interested in the job. Three more would be perfect. If you know anyone. Since we'll be living and working in close quarters aboard the spaceship, it's not a bad idea for you to pick friends."

Yvette could think of a few classmates who might be interested. The thing was: no matter how ridiculous this job might be, mice who could snag jobs working for otters—or cats, she supposed—were generally set for life afterwards. The exchange rate between societies composed of mice and societies composed of giants—who needed much more material to feed, clothe, and shelter themselves on a daily basis—were generally *extremely* favorable.

Likely, the only reason Kipper had had trouble finding mice to work for her was that she'd been asking mice with established lives and careers. Ones who didn't need a sudden windfall. Ones with something to lose. If Yvette passed along this job offer to some of her friends who were having trouble paying off their college debt—hungry students instead of self-satisfied professors—well... There'd be no problem.

And Yvette could be an astronaut with three chosen friends.

This was a deal too good to pass up.

"I'm in."

CHAPTER 2
SEQUOIA

Sequoia collected stars like other squirrels collected acorns. Not really. Because squirrels didn't collect acorns anymore, except for kits on the playground. And no matter how much Sequoia wanted to gather all the stars in the sky—all the red giants and blue dwarfs; all the pretty yellow and orange ones—up into a pile and bury them deep inside a black hole where they would be hers, all hers and only hers forever and forever, you just can't do that with stars.

But the red squirrel still collected them. She found them, deep in the dark patches of the sky, seeking them out with her telescope, and then she catalogued them, numbering and naming them. She kept them in lists and charts and spreadsheets. She knew them all by heart.

Sequoia mapped out the cosmos. She would be the ideal navigator for an interstellar spacecraft, and she knew it. She hadn't hesitated to accept the job when Kipper offered it to her. It was the perfect job for her. The job she'd been dreaming about her whole life, without even realizing it.

Sequoia had been thinking about moving from Earth up to one of the otter space stations for some time, to be closer to the stars. So, she'd been living lightly, meaning it had been easy to sublet her treetop apartment, sell her thrift store furniture back to the thrift store at a minor loss, and pack up her few sentimental belongings to be stored at her sister's branch house.

She left Treesylvania with nothing but a backpack slung over her shoulder, packed with a few changes of clothes and two laptop computers—one for star-mapping and one for Star Quest, her favorite video game. Which she had written. Because she was awesome and in her spare time, after cataloguing the cosmos, Sequoia programmed and maintained a massively multiplayer online game. The accounts of players were anonymous, but she suspected, based on the locations they signed in from on Deep Sky Anchor and Kelp Frond Station, that most of the fans of her game were otters.

Sequoia expected to get along with her new team mates fine. She would meet most of the team when she got to the Uplifted States. Kipper and Trugger—after the lunch where they'd invited her to join the team—had suggested that she travel with them as a group from Europe to the Uplifted States, after they finished recruiting a few more crewmembers. They'd be flying from New London, so Sequoia took the overnight maglev train and watched her hometown with its towering, tree-like buildings dwindle into the distance behind her, lost among the thick forests of actual trees.

No matter how small the city of Treesylvania looked from the train window—no matter how many forests or mountains; or how much of the Earth's curvature hid it from her—she was still closer to her home than she'd ever been to the stars, even though that was where her heart lived, dancing among the constellations in deep space. She would be there soon. She couldn't wait.

Sequoia slept on the train with her head leaned against the window. When she awoke, the train was slowing, pulling into a station. They'd arrived in New London, and when she stepped out of the train, Kipper and Trugger were waiting for her on the platform. The gray tabby and river otter with his emerald green stripes each stood head and shoulders taller than Sequoia. They held a large, rolling suitcase between them, probably large enough that a squirrel could fit inside, and the river otter had a bulky, squishy-looking, maroon-colored pack strapped to his long back.

They were also wearing their Uplifted States Space Administration uniforms. Navy blue with silver trim, covered in pockets. They looked sharp. "When do I get a fancy uniform?" Sequoia asked. The navy blue would look good against her fiery, red fur.

"Not until we get back to the States," Kipper said.

As Sequoia approached the otter, she got a better look at his backpack. The color shivered, shifting from deep maroon to pale pink, and then a touch of rainbow fluttered across it. The squirrel stopped in her tracks, staring at it. "What is going on with that backpack?"

"Oh, this?" Trugger said. "He's sleeping."

"Who's... what?" Sequoia stared a little longer and realized that the backpack wasn't changing colors at all. It was transparent. There was something coiled up inside of it. Something with twists and curves and lots of little round discs. Something moving with a gentle in and out rhythm. Something... breathing.

"That's Obsidian," Kipper explained. "He's joining us from the octopus city of Polychromia in the Mediterranean Sea. He's a renowned expert in linguistics and should prove invaluable if we encounter any alien species in our travels."

Sequoia blinked, and her tufted red ears twitched. "Aliens? And... do octopuses even speak?" Now that she knew what she was looking at inside the backpack, she could make sense of the coiled-up tentacles with their sucker discs.

"Their language is based on color and movement," Kipper said.

Trugger added dreamily, "Rainbows and dancing..."

Kipper continued: "But some of them—including Obsidian

and any other octopi who interact with otters regularly—also use a simplified sign language that's a variant of Swimmer's Sign. And in Obsidian's case, he has an unusual sensitivity to vibrations, so he can pick up on spoken languages as well. Albeit with limitations. He's been working on developing a computer translation technology that will make it easier for octopi who aren't sensitive enough to vibrations to understand spoken languages to communicate with the rest of us, regardless of whether we know sign language. We're very lucky to have him on the team. Now, about the uniform, yours—like Obsidian's and the mice's—will have to be custom sewn for you once we get to the Uplifted States."

Sequoia had trouble picturing one of the Uplifted States Space Administration uniforms in an octopus shape... She supposed she'd have to wait and see what that looked like.

"Come on," Kipper said, beginning to pull the giant wheeled suitcase away from the train which still had passengers streaming out of it. The tabby cat led them through the crowd of squirrels and otters on the platform, heading toward the exit to New London's streets. "We have four more team members to pick up before heading to the airport. It won't be a long walk."

There were train stations all over New London, and Sequoia had got off the train at the station closest to Mousfordshire. She followed the tabby cat and river otter along the New London streets, marveling as she always did when in New London at how different the city—built within the ruins of an ancient human city—was from Treesylvania, which had been constructed entirely by squirrels, for squirrels, well after the Dark Times when humans had disappeared from the Earth.

Treesylvania had been carved freshly out of the forests around Transylvania, and all the buildings were designed to look and feel tree-like. Perfectly and specifically designed for squirrels. Here, in New London, many of the buildings had been adapted from the towering monuments to humanity that still remained. Giant, cavernous, stone monstrosities, far too large for the otters who now lived in them. So, the buildings had been bisected, and smaller, more practical buildings had been built inside of and around them. It was a city on two scales: human and otter.

Dizzyingly, the scale changed to include a third default size, as they entered the tiny, footpath-like streets of Mousfordshire. The two-story mouse buildings stood twice as tall as the tips of Sequoia's tufted ears. One-story buildings were shorter than her. She felt like she was walking through a toy store display room filled with giant doll houses.

Above the whole city rose the giant clock tower, Big Ben, which the mice had, miraculously, kept running all these years, keeping perfect time. And bordering the eastern side of Mousfordshire ran the Thames, a perfect, glittering blue river, wider than the mouse city itself, and filled with bobbing boats, some staked to the shoreline and others floating along. Many of the boats had kiosks on them, and otters wearing fast-dry clothes swam up to the kiosks to buy food or do other business. It was a city of its own sort, flowing along with the river.

Kipper and Trugger came to an apartment building—nearly three times Sequoia's height—with tiny balconies under all the windows. The tabby leaned down and—with a carefully extended claw—delicately pressed a tiny buzzer beside the front door. A few moments later, a mouse emerged. Three more mice followed after her, and introductions were made all around. Except for Obsidian, who was still sleeping on Trugger's back, and the mice didn't seem to notice him.

The first mouse, Yvette, had gray fur, much the same color as Kipper's stripes. The next one had an apricot tinge to her fur and was called Josie. Wendell had tiny white splotches patching his brown fur, and Mulberry was colored like a Siamese cat—dark muzzle and ears, white fur otherwise. They all had dark, bright eyes, and twitchy noses graced with whiskers so thin and fine that Sequoia could barely see them.

Kipper and Trugger opened the giant rolling suitcase they'd been dragging around New London, and inside, it was decked out like a small dormitory—two simple bunk beds, just the size for mice, and it was wired up with an internal light. Sequoia almost laughed at the sight. Here was the dollhouse she'd kept picturing the Mousfordshire houses to be.

As Kipper helped the mice by loading their own miniscule suitcases inside the giant one, she looked like a giant kitten playing with her dolls. It was such a disrespectful way for Sequoia to see her new colleagues that she clapped her paws against her muzzle, afraid she'd say something that would betray her thoughts.

Sequoia wondered how hard it would be for the mice to get by when they got to the Uplifted States. It couldn't be easy to be that small in a world designed by and for dogs and cats. Mostly dogs, from what Sequoia understood. She found herself feeling almost smug about her own size. Sure, she was smaller than Kipper and Trugger, but she'd be big enough to get around on her own. Besides, squirrels are built for climbing. If something was out of reach, she could probably find a way to scamper up to any high cupboards.

The feeling faded the further that the group travelled. Walking through New London, Sequoia felt perfectly comfortable. The otters they passed who lived there treated her no differently than she'd ever been treated. But after they'd taken a car from the edge of Mousfordshire to the airport, they started encountering more and more tourists, mostly dogs. And Sequoia felt them watching her. Dogs turned their heads as she walked by. Dogs stared at her, long after they should have. They paid more attention to her than Trugger's color-changing backpack, stuffed full of tentacles.

As they sat in the terminal, waiting to board their transatlantic flight, Sequoia fidgeted with the jacket and blouse she was wearing, wondering if they were too flashy somehow. There were constellations sewn into the fabric of the jacket, made from tiny crystal buttons, and they sparkled prettily in the light. But then, she flicked her tail, nervously, and a dog sitting across the way got up. She was a medium-sized, brown-furred dog. Sequoia didn't know dog breeds well enough to be sure of more than that.

The dog came straight towards Sequoia, paws folded together in front of her, and said, "I just think you should know that you have the prettiest fluffy red tail. It looks like fire!"

"Uh... thanks," Sequoia said, reflexively folding her tail around herself, making it less visible.

"Oh, don't do that!" the dog said. Standing so close, she seemed very large. "Your tail's so beautiful, don't ever hide it."

"Excuse me," Kipper said, getting up and placing herself between the dog and the squirrel. "But my team and I need to discuss some important business before boarding the plane."

"We do?" Sequoia asked, only catching onto what was happening a moment after the words escaped her muzzle.

"Yes, we do," Kipper said, firmly. To the dog, she added, "Could you give us some privacy? Thank you so much."

The dog went away, muttering something about rude cats and ungrateful squirrels.

Kipper ran her paws down the front of her navy tunic. "Holy haddock, I love this uniform. Dogs never listened to me that easily when I wore street clothes."

"That was easy?" Sequoia asked. Her tail—which apparently was beautiful and looked like fire, enough so to be worth remarking on it—was still wrapped tightly around herself, held unnaturally still.

"Unfortunately, yes," Kipper said, sitting back down beside Sequoia. "I'm afraid you may see a lot of that in the Uplifted States."

Sequoia looked around the terminal and realized that some-where between New London's streets and here, the balance had changed so thoroughly that the only otters left seemed to be wearing airline uniforms. Everyone else was dogs. All different sizes and shapes of dogs. Floppy eared, pointy eared; shaggy furred, sheer furred; hulking huge, small as a cat. But even the smallest were bigger than Sequoia. She wasn't large for a squir-rel, but she was very small surrounded by dogs.

When the airplane was ready, and they filed onto it, single file, she started to realize just how much smaller she was. The dogs in front of and behind her loomed over her. When she got to her seat and tried to load her backpack into the overhead bin, a dog stopped her from climbing up on her seat to reach. He helped, by taking the backpack from her paws and lifting it out of her reach, without even asking if that was okay.

As Sequoia watched Kipper and Trugger secure their giant suitcase into one of the seats, she began to envy the mice their tiny refuge inside, all done up like a dormitory. They didn't have to deal with the dogs out here at all. Staring at her, whispering about her, and now that she thought about it, asking her repeat-edly if she had her boarding pass, knew where she was going, needed any help, was in the right place... It was almost like they'd just been coming up with excuses to come talk to her ever since she'd entered the airport. Sequoia hadn't noticed until now, but they hadn't been doing that to Kipper nearly as much. Or Trugger at all.

Sequoia closed her eyes and curled up in the airplane seat that was too large for her to sit on with her feet on the floor. She kept her eyes closed as the airplane took off, imagining that it was a spaceship, and they weren't just flying into the sky but beyond it.

Sequoia wasn't sure she wanted to go to the Uplifted States. But she was ready to head straight out to the stars.

Then she heard Kipper whisper something to Trugger that

turned her heart cold. The cat, sitting in the seat beside her, probably thought Sequoia was asleep; her eyes had been closed for a long time.

"Let's get home and get this mission in the air before the new president can cancel our funding."

The stars had never felt farther away.

CHAPTER 3
AMELIA

The Lucky Boomerang squatted on the tarmac like a half-melted scramball. The name of the spaceship had been hotly contested for a few months while it was being built—a lot of dogs and cats had wanted to name it *The Lucky Frisbee* for the flying disc-shaped toys, because deep in the cultural consciousness of the Uplifted States, spaceships were still expected to be flying saucers. Even though they never were. Even *The Lucky Boomerang* was only vaguely disc-shaped, and that was largely because the committee who had approved the hull design had added non-functional wings to either side. For aesthetic reasons.

'Aesthetic reasons' were also cited when a team of dogs showed up to paint the hull with lime green hexagons, outlined in dark silver—the colors of a regulation scramball. The hexagons got kind of droopy around the edges, but Amelia thought it looked good. Cheerful and fun.

In the end, though, an influential First Racer preacher, fomenting opposition to the space program, had conceded that a spaceship might be alright, as long as all the Good Dogs and Nice Cats remembered that humans had intended them to stay on Earth. Thus, the spaceship had been named for a flying toy known for coming back.

Amelia straightened the tunic of her new, navy blue Uplifted States Space Administration uniform. Her ivory curls flowed over the crisp collar and puffed out at the ends of the sleeves. She'd been letting her fur grow long lately. She liked the way her curls flopped over her eyes, shielding her from the world and keeping others from feeling on solid footing with her, since they couldn't make out her expression beneath her fur.

It always seemed to make others nervous when they couldn't quite see the eyes of the person they were talking to. Amelia kind of liked it. She didn't need to look at other dogs'—or cats'—eyes to read more information about them—from their posture, their tone of voice, their tiny gestures and stance—than she wanted to know.

Most dogs with long fur kept it trimmed short around their eyes. And sure, Amelia could see better right after a trim. But she liked the advantage of putting others on edge better. And shielding herself.

The airlock of *The Lucky Boomerang* was wide open, both inner and outer doors, and the gangplank was lowered to the tarmac, so Amelia had no trouble getting aboard. Security wasn't really an issue once someone got as close to the spaceship as the tarmac. It was getting inside the facility surrounding the tarmac that was the hard part. But Amelia had been assigned to this mission.

The captain and rest of the crew just didn't know about her yet. But she was one of them now. A late addition—and possibly unwanted—but a full member with a uniform and everything.

Amelia walked through the corridors of the ship, heading toward the bridge. She was familiar with its layout from the blueprints. The corridors were a comfortable size for her, as she was only a little taller than most cats. A tall dog like a greyhound or Great Dane would have had to hunker over uncomfortably in some places. That would need to be fixed in future models.

Assuming there were future models.

Amelia had her doubts about this entire project.

The doctrine of the First Race said that dogs should wait patiently for humans to return. Good Dogs waited. This meant that all of the rich dogs throwing money at this ill-conceived government project were either poor First Racers or just really bad at understanding the doctrines that they themselves believed in. Either way, Amelia didn't see any harm in some fun while canine-kind waited. A quick jaunt out to the next few solar systems was basically a walk around the block writ large. And you couldn't expect a dog not to take herself on a few walks while waiting. Even a Good Dog.

Amelia headed to the bridge of the ship first, but no one was there. The main viewscreen was dark; all the workstations were empty; and the only sound was a soft hum. Amelia wondered if that meant the engines were running. They shouldn't be ready for takeoff yet, but it was possible the engineers were running tests.

Next, Amelia made her way to the engine room where she found four mice, an octopus, and a squirrel playing cards in the middle of the floor while the cats and dogs worked around them. Not exactly professional behavior.

The octopus was wearing breathing gear in the form of translucent bulbs of water on either side of his mantle. Unlike the others, he didn't wear a uniform—just wristbands around a few of his tentacles in the colors of the others' uniforms, navy blue with silver edging. He was sitting in a low pan of water to keep himself from drying out, which seemed like a clear safety hazard to Amelia.

Most of the octopus's dimpled, wrinkly skin glistened with moisture but had been kept bare, probably to aide in his ability to communicate using colors. Right now, he had taken on a splotchy coloring that seemed to resemble a hodgepodge of hearts, clubs, spades, and diamonds in black and red, speckling his ashy gray skin. Mimicking the cards.

Amelia wondered idly if the octopus changed his patterning in purposeful ways to bluff the other players into thinking he had good or poor hands.

The mice were barely bigger than the cards laying face down on the floor in front of them. Their hands of cards were too big to comfortably hold them up for long. One of the mice kept awkwardly lifting her cards up to peer at them without letting the others see.

Amelia shook her head and sighed. She didn't like that the cat in charge of this program had insisted on including outsiders in the project. Sure, she'd read all the briefs explaining how each one of the crew members was absolutely necessary—including that ridiculous otter who served as second in command. At least, he *had* served as second in command, until now. Amelia hoped Captain Brighton wouldn't take it too badly when she saw the paperwork reassigning Diplomatic Observer Amelia von Cupsworth to take over as second in command. It would be good if she could have a professional working relationship with the captain. However, she didn't care how the otter took it. From what she'd seen, he had zero real credentials, and Captain Brighton had brought him aboard purely out of nepotism and poorly placed friendship.

Amelia had concerns about a feline captain—or really any cat —who picked her friends so poorly. There was nothing wrong with nepotism when it was used to raise up the right Good Dogs and Nice Cats. But a space pirate otter? He had no place in the Uplifted States, let alone their brand new space program. Otters were unpredictable rogues at the best of times, and these were not the best of times, what with all the cats in the land getting ideas about their superiority from the fluke where Captain Brighton's brother won a single stint as president.

The red squirrel put down her hand of cards, peered at Amelia—probably trying and failing to catch the dog's eye, due to the fringe of curly fur covering them—and said, "Excuse me, but do you need some help? You look lost, and... where did you get that uniform? Are you a new crew member? I thought, I'd already met everyone."

The squirrel stood up and her tail flicked alluringly behind her. Amelia had to hold back a snarl. The squirrel should control that tail better, and ideally keep it tucked entirely out of sight. It was much too distracting. "Yes," Amelia woofed through clenched teeth, "I've been assigned to this crew as a diplomatic observer and first officer." She held out a paw, stiffly, formally. "Commander Amelia von Cupsworth. You must be... Sequoia Birch?"

The squirrel laughed—a chittering, musical sound that felt like rainbows dancing all over under Amelia's skin. She shook off the feeling as fast as she could, setting her jaw, and frowning at the squirrel.

"And why, may I ask, is that funny?" Amelia woofed.

The squirrel gave her a crooked smile, a charmingly lopsided expression on her finely featured face. "Well, I'm the only squirrel onboard. So, not a hard guess, right? Even if you didn't know from the crew profiles that Sequoia Birch was a squirrel, it's a pretty safe bet from the name, right? Two types of tree?"

One of the mice said, "I have a cousin named Magnolia Larch."

Another mouse said, "Didn't we meet a dog named Willow Spruce at the airport while going through customs?"

Amelia grumbled, feeling a fool. She couldn't tell if the mice were making fun of her—making up names for fictional cousins and customs workers—or if they really did know mice and dogs with double tree names. She wasn't good at reading sarcasm and knew that she tended to take things more literally than most dogs. And yet, it was still possible that the cousin and customs worker were real.

Amelia had heard that squirrels were good at making fools of dogs, and now this squirrel had a whole card game's worth of mice laughing at her. She was glad for the fringe of curls, half covering her eyes. She'd have to watch this squirrel carefully.

"Where's Captain Brighton?" Amelia asked gruffly, trying to cut through the tinkling laughter of the tiny mice. Even the octopus's colors were rippling in a way that looked like it might be laughter now.

"Captain Brighton and... uh... Officer Trugger are working on cutting through some bureaucratic red tape... I mean, doing some paperwork in the barracks," Sequoia said. The way she said "Captain Brighton" left Amelia one hundred percent sure that the foolish cat had her subordinates calling her by her first name most of the time. That was no way to keep order.

"Thank you," Amelia said curtly. "Now, please clear out of the way here. This is no way to run an engine room."

"Excuse me?" one of the mice squeaked. She had pale orange fur. From the crew manifest that Amelia had studied, she knew this one was named Josie Longtail.

"You heard me, Officer Longtail. Get this mess cleared off the floor." Amelia waved a paw dismissively at the card game.

The octopus, Obsidian, turned into a dark purple mass of writhing tentacles. He looked angry and started making complicated gestures with the tentacles that weren't holding his hand of cards. Belatedly, Amelia realized he was speaking sign language to her. "What's Officer Obsidian saying?" she asked.

More laughter from the mice and squirrel.

Sequoia said in amazement, "They assigned a dog to help command this crew who doesn't speak Swimmer's Sign?"

At this point, one of the dogs working on the engine—a skinny dachshund with short dark fur—took an interest in the conversation going on in the middle of the room. "Hey guys, lay off the new dog. Most dogs and cats in the Uplifted States don't learn sign language." He stuck out a paw toward Amelia. "I'm Freddy."

Amelia considered correcting Freddy and calling him by his title and last name... but it was becoming increasingly clear that she'd be fighting a losing battle here against the casual culture that Captain Brighton had chosen to foster. Instead, she sighed, shook his paw, and asked, "So do you know what the octopus is saying?"

"I've only picked up a little of Swimmer's Sign so far, but from what I've picked up, I don't think you want to hear it." As the dachshund spoke, his paws fluttered, gesturing in complicated, dancing patterns.

Amelia frowned. "If you only know a few words of Swimmer's Sign, how come you're signing so much?"

"Oh this?" Freddy asked. "This is MSL—Mericka Sign Language. I've been using it since I was a pup, because my brother, Georgie, is deaf." He gestured over a shoulder at the other, plumper dachshund. "It's a different sign language, but there are some similarities. I'll be the first to admit that it gives both Georgie and me a real head start on learning Swimmer's Sign. But I'm sure you'll catch up. The cats are doing great."

"The cats...?" Amelia asked, feeling like she was having trouble keeping up on a number of levels. "What about the squirrel and mice?"

"*The squirrel and mice,*" Sequoia said in a tone that made it perfectly clear that she didn't think much of being referred to by her species instead of her name, "already know Swimmer's Sign, because just about everyone in Europe learns it."

"Well, this isn't a European space program," Amelia snapped. She hadn't read anything about sign language—either Swimmer's Sign or MSL—being such an important aspect of communication among the crew of *The Lucky Boomerang* in the progress reports from Captain Brighton. She wondered what else the cat had been leaving out. "Now, as I commanded before, get this card game cleared up and out of the way."

None of the card players moved.

After an awkward silence, Freddy said, "I'm going to have to respectfully ask, Commander von Cupsworth, that you don't interfere with how we're running the engine room." He gestured at the other canine and feline officers—a calico cat; a tabby-point Siamese; and the dachshund who looked a lot like him, but less skinny—working on the control panels and twisting pipes lacing the edge of the room. "Hedda, Katasha, Georgie and I can't crawl into the loopy piping structures that the epsilon drive engine requires, so we need our smaller officers available at a moment's notice to help us out. If they clear out and go somewhere else, it will slow our progress down whenever we need them to crawl inside the piping and check something out."

The calico cat called out, without turning away from the open panel she was wiring, "Besides, I have twenty bucks riding on the outcome of that game."

Amelia frowned again. She didn't like that the chief engineer was a cat when she read about it in the files, and now she liked it even less. A feline captain was more than enough cat leadership for one crew.

Clearly, if Amelia wanted to pull this crew into shape, she'd need to start changing the culture from the top down. And that meant dealing with Captain Brighton.

CHAPTER 4
YVETTE

As soon as the scruffy white dog insisting she was the ship's new second in command left the engine room, Josie signed with her delicate hand-like paws, "That is one grumpy mop of fur."

Obsidian's color shifted from the angry shade of plum he'd become to a self-satisfied shade of soft peach. He signed with the tips of three tentacles—which grew so thin at the very ends that they weren't much larger than a mouse's paw: "I'll believe she's second in command when Captain Kipper tells us so. Besides, I'm here as an independent advisor, directly from the octopus oligarchy. I don't answer to dog politicians."

Like most mice, Yvette had been taught to understand the octopus counterparts of the otter signs in Swimmer's Sign during school, but before this mission, she'd never seen an octopus signing them in person. Obsidian's tentacles moved with such grace and elegance that it made the otter half of the dual-sign language—the one she could perform with her own paws—feel like a simplified, pidgin version. Like trying to sing the melody of a song that really ought to be performed by a string quartet.

"That's fine for you," Wendell said. He was the mouse with

white speckles on brown fur, and he wasn't getting the same kick out of practicing Swimmer's Sign as Josie and Mulberry seemed to be. "I'm sure an octopus and a squirrel can book flights on an airplane out of here with no problem if this program goes belly up. But—"

They'd had this argument before.

Yvette cut him off, speaking and trying to sign along as she did: "Stop, Wendell. Just stop. I've told you that Commander Trugger has taken personal responsibility for getting us back to New London if there are any problems. We're not going to get stuck, forgotten in some room with doors too big for us to open until we starve."

"Besides, if it came to that," Sequoia chittered, "Obsidian and I would bring you with us. You won't get abandoned in the Uplifted States."

Grumbling, Wendell picked up his hand of cards and hid behind them, an effective blockade given their size relative to him. He was the mouse struggling most with living among cats and dogs, possibly partly because he'd never been as close of a friend with Yvette, Josie, and Mulberry as they were with each other. At least, Yvette and Josie used to be close, before the apricot-colored mouse had taken first place in three competitions at the same gymnastics meet and quit gymnastics altogether, convincing Mulberry to quit with her. The two of them had joined an architecture firm right after graduating college. That's where they'd met Wendell. He was older and didn't have a background in gymnastics, but he'd been an engineer who'd worked on restoring Big Ben and ran marathons on the weekends.

Yvette told herself that she'd drifted apart from her best friend Josie—and consequently Mulberry—because they were spending their time so differently. Not because she was jealous of Josie's three gold medals. Not that. Surely, not that. She wasn't that petty. Really, she wasn't.

Of course, Josie probably wouldn't believe her if she

explained that time was all that had come between them. Yvette wasn't sure she believed it herself.

The card game advanced a few rounds. Hedda the calico made her twenty bucks when Obsidian won again. And then Freddy came to the group to say, "Okay, time for work. I need three of you to run the pipes again and check for where the beam's getting stuck."

That meant mice. Both Sequoia and Obsidian could fit into the pipes, but they couldn't run through them efficiently.

Yvette laid down her cards and said, "Count me in. This hand is terrible." It wasn't, but she loved running the pipes and didn't care about the card game.

Josie, Mulberry, and Wendell looked at each other warily and then burst into several rapid rounds of rock-paper-scissors, pounding their paws in rhythm and either whooping or sighing at the result, until it was determined that Josie could keep playing cards.

Wendell and Mulberry would run the pipes with Yvette.

"Which pipes do you want checked?" Mulberry asked.

Freddy pointed to two pipes near the floor and one near the ceiling.

"I call ceiling!" Yvette said and ran off before the others could object. Not that they would. The piping in the floor coiled much less tightly than in the ceiling. Mulberry claimed the tight turns made her dizzy, and Wendell simply preferred running long distances, more like the marathons he was used to. And fair enough. He was really fast at it.

Whereas, Yvette liked the feeling of constantly twisting and turning. It brought back some of her favorite parts of being a gymnast. Somehow, she never seemed to get dizzy.

Tiny ladder railings were built into all the walls of the engine room, making it possible for Yvette to scurry up to the opening of the pipe on her own. Though, it would get even easier once they were in space. She was really looking forward to experiencing zero gravity. She wanted to try out some of her favorite gymnastics routines and see how well they adapted.

Of course, she wouldn't have the usual parallel bars and balance beams to work with, but she thought she'd probably be able to do some interesting things with the ladders and pipes. She would miss having the creativity and aesthetic sense of her trainer and choreographer to help her... but she'd be able to come up with some routines herself. She'd still have fun.

The mouth of the pipe was nothing to the cats and dogs on the crew—just a hole that they could maybe reach their paws into. To Yvette, though, it was a yawning cave, and every time she stepped inside it, she felt like she was beginning an adventure.

"I'm turning on the beam now," Freddy woofed.

Yvette held out her paw, reaching for the exact middle of the pipe, and waved it around until she found the red laser beam. A wide red dot lit up her paw, making it glow like something from a fantasy movie. She was the Chosen Mouse, and this was the path to her Glorious Destiny. Yvette craned her neck, bringing her nose just close enough to the harmless beam of light for her to see the bright red shine on her whiskers. It danced with every breath that made the fine filaments of her whiskers quiver in the air. She smiled, but held back the laughter she felt in her heart.

She lived on a spaceship. She worked on a spaceship. And if things went well, they'd soon be in space.

Yvette dropped to all fours and began running along the pipe. She moved faster that way, and though she couldn't compete with Wendell's speed—and didn't want to—she intended to do a good job for the feline and canine engineers building this modern marvel.

At every seam between pieces of pipe, Yvette stopped, held up her paw, and checked that the beam was bending properly along the twisting, curving path. Still centered in the pipe. The pipes themselves were securely welded together, shaped exactly to the specifications for the epsilon drive that the otters had found in the ancient octopus ruins on Europa. However, the beam of light bent according to the epsilon field waves generated by the engine.

The pipes Yvette was running through were merely a track for accelerating particles. It was the invisible, ineffable epsilon waves that would bend the particle beam into following the track so that the sub-atomic particles could zoom around, faster and faster, until their racing pinched the fabric of space, allowing the ship to fold its way instantly from one location to the next, disregarding the limitations imposed by the speed of light.

Yvette liked to imagine that she was a sub-atomic particle herself while she ran through the curlicues of piping. She certainly felt tiny enough, living in this cat and dog world.

The way the pipes twisted made Yvette think of the etchings by the ancient human artist M.C. Escher or maybe a machine by Rube Goldberg. Finally, she came to a seam at a tightly curved point in the piping where the red beam of laser light didn't show up centered. She stopped, waved her paws around, and finally located the beam, near the top of the pipe. She moved her paw back and forth, tracing the beam's path and found that it had stopped curving. She checked the address of the location, etched into the metal of the pipe in the form of a simple five-digit number, along the seam.

"Freddy," Yvette called out, squeaking as loud as she could. "I found the problem."

"Yvette?" His bark echoed through the curves of the pipe, sounding distant and small, like a shadow of his voice back in the engine room.

"That's right. Ready for the address?"

"Ready."

Yvette read the number out and waited for his response. She knew the cats and dogs must be working furiously to figure out what was wrong with the field shape of the epsilon waves, and she didn't mind waiting. Eventually, they'd need her to pull the measuring tape out of her pocket and take more specific measurements as they tried to fix it.

She laid down on the cool, curved metal of the pipe, next to the address etching, and took the end of her tail in her paws. She twirled the end of her tail and watched the circles it made, thinking about how small they were and how much larger the circles were that the planets made around the sun.

She was going to escape those circles in this ship and fly away into the galaxy. The mere idea made her feel light and giddy, as if she could do a triple flip during a gymnastics routine... and instead of plummeting back down to the mat... just soar up into the sky.

CHAPTER 5
KIPPER

As soon as she laid eyes on the curly-furred mop of a dog —bizarrely wearing one of their USSA-specific blue-and-silver uniforms—Kipper could tell that Amelia was not a dog who had any patience for waiting.

The gray tabby cat captain closed the laptop computer that she and Trugger had been working on—writing emails, searching directories for officials who could help them, and downloading form after form that didn't quite fit their situation. Nothing fit their situation. She put the laptop aside and got up from the bottom bunk bed she'd been sitting on. "Can I help you?" she asked the dog.

"Commander Amelia von Cupsworth, reporting for duty," the dog said. She snapped a smart salute with her paw at her brow.

Kipper saluted back, feeling silly. Sure, officers had saluted each other all the time when she'd been aboard *The Jolly Barracuda*, but everything about that ship had been silly. And at some level, all the otters involved—Captain Cod included—had seemed to know it.

This dog didn't look like she'd recognize silliness if she were looking at dictionary definition examples of it.

"It's nice to meet you, Amelia," Kipper said, pointedly using the dog's first name. If she was a commander, she could hardly object to the ship's captain and director of an entire program calling her by her first name. Although, it probably rankled her. Let it. "But we already have a commander on *The Lucky Boomerang*." She smiled, making sure the expression reached all the way into her whiskers, and then she gestured to the river otter with green stripes dyed into his fur, still sitting on the bunk bed built into the barracks wall. "Let me introduce Commander Trugger."

"We're not formal here," Trugger said getting up and sticking out a webbed paw. "You can just call me Trugger."

The mop dog frowned. She shouldered her way out of a backpack, opened it up, and pulled out several pages of paper.

Kipper took the crisp sheets—surprisingly crisp for having been stored in a backpack—and read them over. "I see," she said. "You've been assigned to be my new second in command."

Kipper sighed deeply. The government dogs had been playing games with her ever since her brother Alistair lost the last presidential election. With the new dog president—a particularly mean and prejudiced golden retriever; yes, even golden retrievers with their famously sunny dispositions can be mean and prejudiced—empowering dogs to be their worst selves, it was a constant challenge to simply keep the new space program from being cancelled.

In the scheme of things, an unwanted second in command was nothing. Especially since power hierarchies are largely imaginary—a truth that Kipper had learned from her time aboard *The Jolly Barracuda* that still seemed to blow most dogs' minds.

"Very well, Commander von Cupsworth," Kipper said wearily, but trying her best to sound cheerful. "Welcome to the crew. Your first task is to inform the rest of the crew about Trugger's new promotion."

"Promotion?" Trugger asked, practically bouncing with excitement. He was easily excited.

"Yes, I'm promoting you to be the new... uh... Chief of Crew Operations. It's a role outside the ship's regular power hierarchy, equal in status to my own as captain, except when it comes to questions of... uh... administrative decision making." Kipper had learned to think quickly on her feet while working for Captain Cod as his Ship's Spy, a role he'd invented on the spot for her when she'd had the presence of mind to call herself a spy, something that charmed him so much he'd made her an honorary otter and member of his crew.

"Wait," Amelia said. "Does that put Chief of Crew Operations Trugger... over me in the ship's hierarchy?"

See, imaginary. Hierarchies were all about making people believe that they fit somewhere in a larger structure... even though the structure itself didn't exist.

"Oh, yes, I suppose it does," Kipper said, trying to keep the smile out of her whiskers this time. She couldn't help sounding bemused, and maybe a little pleased with herself. "Imagine that."

Amelia frowned, clearly stymied by Kipper's unorthodox move.

The great thing about dogs, though, was that even the hardest edged, most politically scheming ones generally had a level at which they wanted to appease, please, and make others happy with them. Predictably, Amelia asked, "Is there anything else, possibly more useful, that I could do for you? I understand that you're struggling with some kind of bureaucratic red tape, and I do have connections in the incoming government."

Kipper and Trugger exchanged a glance. The green striped otter shrugged. He didn't know a lot about working with the Uplifted States government. So, this decision was up to Kipper. And honestly, she didn't see how the situation could get a lot worse or more gridlocked than it already was. "Alright," she said, pulling the laptop up from the bunk where she'd left it. She opened it up, clicked to the right window, and turned it toward Amelia. "We're having trouble getting authorization for the last members of our crew to join us."

Even beneath the fringe of curls, Kipper could see Amelia's eyes widen. To her credit, the dog didn't say anything, just kept reading the screen. Once she finished, she frowned, shook her head, and sighed. "Consider it done."

Now Kipper's eyes widened. It was all she could do to stop herself from saying, "Really??? You've got to be kidding!"

Trugger didn't stop himself. "Really??? You've got to be kidding!"

"If you say that this bonded octopus-raptor pair living under asylum on the Europa Base are necessary members of *The Lucky Boomerang's* crew, then they're necessary. I'll get the authorizations taken care of. You don't need to worry about it any more. Do you still want me to tell the rest of the crew about..." She sighed deeply. "...Chief of Crew Operations Trugger's promotion?"

"Uh, yes, thank you," Kipper said. "That would be very helpful."

"They're all in the engine room," Trugger said.

"I know," Amelia replied. "I met them on my way to find you."

"I bet meeting us didn't go the way you expected!" Trugger looked very happy about his promotion. Otters who'd served aboard *The Jolly Barracuda* were strange that way. They both approached hierarchies with a postmodern flexibility, and yet took a genuine delight in the same hierarchies that they turned all topsy turvy, sideways, upside down, and inside out.

"Not exactly, no," Amelia grumbled.

"One more thing before you go," Kipper said. "We'll be ready for our first engine test soon. Do you have everything you'd need for a full space flight?"

Amelia patted the backpack that she'd pulled the crisp papers out of. "Spacesuit, change of uniform, a few personal supplies. Based on what I read about the mission, I should be set."

"It sounds like it," Kipper agreed.

The dog saluted again. Kipper and Trugger saluted back.

Once Amelia was all the way out of the barracks, Kipper said in a low voice, "She knows something. Something we don't."

"You think so?" Trugger asked.

"I'm sure of it. Or she would never have agreed to Nioli and Gy'krr joining the crew at Europa. I don't think she thinks our mission is going to make it that far."

"We'll just have to prove her wrong," Trugger said. "Like a penguin holding its breath."

"Yes," Kipper agreed, having no idea what he meant. "Exactly like a penguin holding its breath." She found it was easier to agree with Trugger's bird metaphors than try to understand or fix them. She'd tried fixing them before... it usually just inspired Trugger to throw more bizarre bird metaphors at her, until they were going around in more and more crowded circles of metaphorical birds. "We need to get this ship off the ground as soon as possible. Once we're in space... the whole game changes."

"May I respectfully suggest then..." Trugger said, folding his webbed front paws together. He looked very handsome in his blue and silver uniform, and a little like an alien from the television space drama Tri-Galactic Trek with his fur dyed into green stripes. "...that we change the goal? If we keep pushing for authorization to make a test flight to Europa, then the government dogs will keep pushing back. But if we ask for authorization for a test flight to the moon..."

"...then suddenly we're not trying to fly off into threatening, contested space, right next to a gas giant filled with hostile raptors and enigmatic octopi," Kipper said, completing his thought. "We're just taking a victory lap around our own planet and demonstrating that dogs—"

"—and cats," Trugger added.

"—yes, yes, of course, *and cats* can get to Moonville Funpark under the power of their own technology. Not threatening."

"Maybe... patriotic?" Trugger asked.

"That spin does seem like it would go over better with the incoming administration."

Trugger reached for the laptop, still in Kipper's paws. He took it and said, "Come on, let's write a proposal, and get our flock flying."

Nobody had a better friend than Trugger.

CHAPTER 6
YVETTE

Months of waiting turned into a week of hurried rushing, seemingly over one restless, sleepless night. All at once, Hedda declared the epsilon engine ready for field testing, and Captain Kipper handed out schedules to everyone. Their amorphous days of playing cards on the engine room floor while occasionally consulting on the designs were through. And suddenly, they were busy dawn to dusk with last minute health checkups, itemizing the onboard supplies to make sure nothing was missing, and most bizarrely —press events.

Yvette was used to being filmed at gymnastics meets, not just while performing but also before and after. Interviewers always wanted to know how she felt—*was she nervous about performing? Excited? Disappointed that she hadn't come in first? Relieved that it was over? What were her plans next? Would she keep competing? Keep trying for that elusive first-place medal?*

Yvette had practiced answering questions like those grace-fully for years. She knew exactly how to reluctantly admit that she was disappointed while carefully counterbalancing her disappointment with gushing happiness and excitement for her competitors who truly deserved their wins. Really, their performances had just been wonderful, top notch, and no one could feel bad about coming in second to such excellence.

But the questions were different here. None of that barely-disguised pity as the reporters tiptoed around saying, "You *lost*; how does that make you *feel*???"

It was hard to believe at first... but the dogs and cats of the press here were treating Yvette like the star of the whole show. Sure, the entire crew was lined up for the press, arranged at a long table with microphones for everyone; all four mice had tiny chairs on top of the table, arranged around a single gigantic microphone, nearly the size of a curled-up mouse. But after a few pointed questions for Captain Kipper and Commander Trugger; cursory questions for Hedda, Katasha, Freddy, and George; and some outright weird, creepy questions for Sequoia (mostly about whether she thought her beautiful tail would get in her way during zero gee); all the press wanted to do was listen to Yvette tell her story about Kipper and Trugger recruiting her, how she'd picked the other mice for the team, and what it was like to know she'd be one of the first moustronauts. (Apparently ignoring all the mice who already lived on otter space stations.) She told the story over and over again, at every one of the events, to dogs, cats, and even a sea otter man, all eagerly pointing cameras at her.

Sure, they probably would have focused on Obsidian, if the octopus had been there. But Obsidian didn't do press events. He invoked his independent contractor status, as well as the physical discomfort involved in spending extra time out in the open air, in order to stay back aboard the ship in his personal aquarium.

So, the reporters treated Yvette like a star. She'd never felt like that before. She'd always been second best, being asked questions that were really, indirectly about the competitors who'd beaten her, when it came down to it.

Several times during the press events for *The Lucky Boomerang*, newscasters introduced Yvette as a "repeated gymnastics champion," as if the difference between her second and third place medallions in silver and bronze and the actual gold medals she'd craved so badly had never mattered at all. She was the only one who seemed to remember or care that she'd never actually won first place. Those distinctions all got erased inside the expansiveness of the simple term "champion."

Yvette had always thought of Josie as the champion between the two of them, with her first-place medal that had given her a ticket out of competing anymore. Of course, Yvette could have quit competing any time too. She didn't need a first-place medal to give her permission. Not really. But she hadn't quit. And somehow, her string of second and third place wins had added up to counting for more in these reporters' eyes than a single gold.

Showing up consistently counted for more than winning first place.

Something deep inside of Yvette was soothed by that knowledge. Something petty and competitive, maybe. But still, something that was a part of her. Something that drove her forward and kept her going. Something that had kept her competing, even when it looked like she'd never win.

Maybe keeping going was enough. Maybe it was showing up that mattered most of all.

"Thanks for handling the press for us," Mulberry said shyly after the mike was turned off at their final event. "I never could handle reporters with all their pushy questions. It's part of why I quit gymnastics when I did. I liked the actual jumping and flipping... but all those cameras? All those faces staring at me? Expecting me to say words without putting my foot in my mouth?" The white mouse with dark markings on her paws and face shuddered, huddling deeper into her tiny chair. "I might be graceful in the air, but I am decidedly not graceful when I have to, you know, *talk* about it."

Yvette shrugged dismissively, and said, "It's nothing really," before catching herself, remembering to stay graceful with her words, and adding, "But you're welcome. I'm happy to do it. I have a lot of practice after all those years I spent chasing the gold."

Josie snorted, but she didn't have time to say anything. A dog came and asked them all to vacate their tiny chairs. He collected the mike and chairs they'd been sitting using, carrying the whole collection of four chairs in his paws at once, while other dogs folded up chairs from the audience. The audience chairs—which had been mostly for dogs and cats—were much larger, and the dogs could only carry one or maybe two at a time, folded and tucked under each arm.

Wendell shook his head. "It's so strange living among giants."

"You don't notice it as much on the *Boomerang*," Josie agreed. "Sure, there are more giants than—" She gestured at the other three mice. "—us. But we're still a significant fraction of the crew, and the whole place is set up to accommodate us. Make us feel normal. Like equal members."

Just as the dogs finished clearing the folding chairs from the room and started eyeing the table where the mice were still standing, Trugger came over and asked, "Anyone want a ride?" He tapped his shoulder.

"I don't mind running," Wendell said, hopping down from the table.

The car they'd come in was just outside the building, but the building was big. Mulberry hesitated a moment and then grinned big. "Actually, I think I'll run too." She'd been racing with Wendell a lot lately. She always lost, but the practice was increasing her speed. She was getting close to catching up with him, and Yvette had to admit it looked like good exercise.

Even so, when Josie said, "Yeah, I'll take a ride," and hopped on Trugger's extended paw, Yvette decided to go with her.

Yvette and Josie sat on Trugger's shoulders, one on each side, while he strode jauntily through the building, rudder tail swaying behind him. The other two mice raced each other at his feet. The rest of the crew—cats, dogs, and squirrel—followed behind at a leisurely pace.

Yvette wanted to ask Josie about whatever it was she'd been about to say... but it was too strange with an otter head between them. You can't have a private conversation with someone when you're both riding on the shoulders of a giant. And yet, if there was anyone who would be understanding about an awkward conversation happening on his shoulders—and maybe even capable of making it less awkward by interjecting some esoteric bird metaphor—that otter was Trugger.

So, Yvette leaned forward and peered across the otter's navy blue collar at her friend. "Was there something you wanted to say to me back there?" she asked, trying to sound casual.

"What?" Josie asked, sounding startled.

"About chasing the gold," Yvette clarified. "When I said I'd been chasing the gold... you, I don't know, snorted? It seemed like you had something to say to me."

After a few moments of awkward silence, Trugger interjected, "Sometimes a snort is just a snort. Like a feather is just a feather. No meaning behind it at all."

"Thank you, Trugger," Josie said, "but in this case, Yvette is right."

Yvette's stomach turned cold and hard at those words. She'd asked for this. But she wasn't sure she actually wanted to hear it —hear Josie tell her off for her pettiness.

"I... still feel..." Josie said slowly and haltingly, before finishing in a quick rush, "...guilty that I won the gold medal that I knew you wanted. You wanted it so much more than I did. I just wanted us to be friends. And then... I ruined it. Because I felt so guilty, I kept pulling away from you. I'm so sorry."

"What?" Yvette said, trying to deal with her understanding

of the last few years turning upside down. She was used to turning upside down physically. Not emotionally. "I thought... I pulled away."

"What?" Josie exclaimed in surprise. "You kept reaching out. Inviting me to lunch or just leaving little messages telling me about what you were up to. I'm the one who was always... pretending to be busy. I thought for sure you'd win a gold of your own, and then all the awkwardness would be over..."

"But I didn't," Yvette said simply. There should have been shame or bitterness in the words, but they were just facts. Now she felt even weirder about how much she'd wanted to win a gold medal, because apparently, if she'd won one, she'd have gotten her friend back? That was messed up.

Or maybe, if she'd just been able to get over her intense desire for one of those shiny gold medals—really get over it— she could have had this conversation with Josie long ago.

"This is heavy," Trugger said.

Each mouse looked at him quizzically, pinning him with enquiry from either side.

"Oh, not literally," he explained. "You're still both quite light. I mean the conversation you're having. Friendship! Competition! Estrangement! That's a lot to be dealing with. It's good you're shaking it out of your feathers now. Gotta be light as the heart of a singing songbird for our takeoff tomorrow."

Trugger didn't say it directly, because his way was to obfuscate everything with bird metaphors. But he was right. The two mice didn't need this argument between them while flying a brand new proto-type starship.

Maybe it was the impending weight of their first flight that had made old arguments and grudges too heavy to bear anymore.

"I'm sorry that I coveted your gold medal so much," Yvette said, feeling lighter as the words left her. It was hard to apologize for simply being the person she'd been. But she wanted to be better. And that was the first step.

"So... we can be friends again?" Josie asked, a quaver in her voice.

"Aren't we already?" Yvette would have said more, expounding on how wonderful it had been working together and playing cards together the last few weeks. But Trugger took a sudden, sharp turn around a corner, ducking into a nook next to a stairwell, off the path that the rest of the crew continued following.

The otter reached up with his paws, offering one webbed paw to each mouse, and tentatively, Yvette and Josie stepped onto the fuzzy platforms.

Trugger brought the two mice around to where all three of them—otter, gray mouse, and orange mouse—could look each other in the eye.

"This is a beautiful moment," he said, "really it is. And I love seeing beautiful moments like this happen. Friendship is so important."

The otter paused. Neither mouse had ever seen him look this serious. He was the levity to Kipper's responsibility. Yet here, his round, bewhiskered face was set with complete gravity.

"But...?" Yvette asked, faltering in the face of his solemn expression.

"But I need to know that you can work together and that—whatever state your friendship is in—you are capable of staying professional during our upcoming mission."

"Our half day mission to the moon and back?" Josie asked, tilting her head and squinting like she was trying to discern what the big deal could possibly be. "We've been working together just fine for weeks," she added. "Why would a half day mission be such a big deal?"

Trugger chewed his whiskers, gaze darting from side to side

nervously. "I can't say, but... you need to be ready. Space is big and dangerous, and you have to take that seriously."

"Okay," Yvette said. Then she looked at Josie who still looked confused. She held out a paw, and Josie held her paw up too, like the orange mouse was a mirror of the gray one. Trugger moved his own paws closer together, close enough that the two mice could clasp their own tiny hand-like paws together. "We're okay, and we're ready to go into space. Aren't we?"

"It's the biggest adventure in the world," Josie agreed.

"Bigger than the world," Yvette said, a grin spreading her whiskers wide.

The grin spread contagiously from Yvette to Josie and finally to Trugger.

"Good!" the otter said. "Because... look... I *can't* say. But you need to be ready." He clearly wanted to tell them something.

"If it's about the mission," Yvette said, "then we'll find out soon enough, right?"

"Right," Trugger agreed, nodding. "Tomorrow can't come soon enough." Then he put the mice back on his shoulders and hop-skipped to catch up with the rest of the crew, heading back to *The Lucky Boomerang*.

CHAPTER 7
AMELIA

That night, the crew of *The Lucky Boomerang* bunked down in the barracks, like they had every other night for weeks. They needed to sleep. They needed to be sharp for their mission in the morning.

But none of them could. Sleep was an ethereal concept. Something they could remember; something that happened every day; and yet seemed impossibly out of reach. Impossible to attain. And some of the crew wasn't even trying.

Amelia listened to the mice squeak and giggle to each other in their corner of the barracks—a dollhouse-sized nook, close to the floor and right to the side of the entrance to the room. It was placed there so the mice wouldn't have to travel all the way to the far end of the room—the equivalent of one of their city blocks in Mousfordshire—to get to their bunks.

Occasionally, Captain Kipper half-heartedly shushed the room, which Amelia respected. But it also revealed that the captain couldn't sleep either.

They were all so nervous. It was a simple flight, from what Amelia understood. And they all seemed to trust the arcane octopus engineering behind the ship implicitly. So, what were they all so worried about?

Amelia grumbled, huffed, and rolled onto her side, trying to shut the sounds of all the restless sleepers out of her floppy ears. She thought longingly of Obsidian's bunk—the only one not in the barracks. As an octopus, he had an enclosed tank of water for sleeping in. Apparently, for safety reasons, it had to be placed closer to the center of the ship. So, Obsidian was the only one not trying to sleep in this shared space, and while Amelia didn't want to sleep in a tank of water, she was jealous of the privacy he got.

In fact, he even got a double-size tank, since it had been designed for including the octopus crew member that Captain Kipper had hoped to pick up on Europa. That wouldn't be happening—sure, Amelia had pulled the strings necessary to get the bonded octopus and raptor included on the crew roster. But this joke of a project would be shut down before it ever made it as far as Europa. The good president Champ Truman would see to that, and then all the Good Dogs of the Uplifted States could get back to life the way it was supposed to be.

Amelia startled at the touch of a paw on her side. She turned and saw in the dark: a small, perfectly formed squirrel face. Ears pointed and nose twitching.

Sequoia whispered to the dog, "I couldn't sleep, and it sounded like you weren't sleeping either."

Amelia's heart pounded at the closeness of the squirrel, and she was glad she couldn't make out the probable flitting of Sequoia's fire-like tail in the darkness. She didn't know how to respond. She could say something about how she had almost been asleep until the squirrel interrupted her, or something about how she didn't understand why everyone was so worked up about tomorrow, or maybe just, why won't those mice stop squeaking? But putting a string of coherent words together took effort, and she didn't do it fast enough.

Sequoia interpreted Amelia's silent stare as agreement, and apparently an invitation, since she crawled into the bunk beside her. Whispering again, this time closer to Amelia's floppy ear, the red squirrel said, "I thought you might like help with your long fur. In zero gee tomorrow, it might get in your way. I could do a few little braids... nothing much, just enough to keep it out of your eyes?"

"I like the hair in my eyes," Amelia muttered, feeling slow and foolish. Her heart was beating quickly though. It was the only quick thing about her right now.

"Even when you could be using your eyes to look at the stars?" Sequoia asked.

The stars were where the First Race had gone.

Amelia's heart stopped racing when she thought of the First Race. The mere thought of the humans who had uplifted dogs and given them this wonderful world to live in was enough to calm her during the worst catastrophes and soothe her through the worst heartbreak. The tension and frustrations aboard this strange vessel and the confusing feelings inspired by a squirrel crawling into her bed beside her were nothing compared to the pervasive happiness of simply thinking about the First Race.

"Okay," Amelia said softly. "You can put in a few braids." She did want to see the stars. She wanted to see them and feel close to the humans, out there, somewhere in the sky.

Amelia wasn't the kind of dog who had the hubris to believe that humans would return during her own lifetime. They would come. The doctrine of the First Race said so. But they had been gone a long time, and the scripture predicting when they would return was... at best... cryptic.

Riding this ridiculous contraption powered by blasphemous octopus technology was probably the closest Amelia would ever come to her beloved humans in the sky. And the squirrel was right: she should keep her eyes clear to see them.

Sequoia worked with dexterous, small paws. She wound locks of Amelia's tawny curls under and over each other, weaving them into tiny plaits above and below the dog's eyes.

She worked so carefully that Amelia could barely feel the gentle tugs on her fur, and yet the activity was almost painfully intimate. The squirrel had to bend so close over Amelia's face, as the dog lay helplessly supine, head resting on her pillow.

When Sequoia was done, she leaned back and said, "There, that's better." The squirrel smiled. "You have very pretty eyes under all those curls."

Amelia looked away bashfully, embarrassed but also confusingly pleased by the squirrel's compliment. Imagine that. Complimented by a squirrel. Then overtaken by curiosity, Amelia sat up in the bed and peered into a small mirror built into the wall beside her bunk. Every bunk had one. It was hard to see in the dark, but the braids looked fancy lining her eyes. Fancy like a squirrel's tail. She felt silly and a little ashamed that she'd let herself be dolled up like this. She felt even sillier realizing how much she liked it.

When Amelia turned back to look at Sequoia and thank her —because thanking her would be polite, and Good Dogs were always polite—the squirrel was already breathing deeply and steadily, sound asleep, with her head on Amelia's pillow.

The scruffy dog's heart jumped again at the sight. A squirrel! Sleeping in her bed! Scandalous! And yet... Sequoia looked so peaceful, and all of them had been struggling to sleep. And they all needed their sleep, tonight more than ever. They needed to perform well for the cameras tomorrow, even if it was only a small mission before the program got shut down.

Amelia decided to let the squirrel keep sleeping beside her, and when the dog laid her own head down on the pillow, she felt the weight of Sequoia's sleep—an emanating drowsiness— pull her down into a surreal patina of dreams, in spite of the mice's continued squeaking and the other cats' and dogs' continued whispering and Captain Kipper's continued hushing. None of it bothered her, not with Sequoia sleeping beside her.

CHAPTER 8
KIPPER

ipper watched the day dawn through *The Lucky Boomerang's* main viewscreen. Everyone else was still asleep. Later in the day, the smart glass of the viewscreen would be filled with readings and calculations, and under those, eventually, stars.

But for now, it was just a window. And through the window, she watched the sky soften through shades of violet and pink into powder blue, decorated with clouds that bled gold and orange. A view that couldn't be seen from space, not like that.

Kipper had come to love living in space. She had spent so much time on *The Jolly Barracuda* with the silly, piratical otters under Captain Cod's command that she'd come to think of the ship as her home, almost as much as any part of Earth. But she'd hated how that spaceship flooded with oxo-agua, making her feel like she was drowning. No, correction, it didn't make her *feel* like she was drowning—*it literally drowned her*, but with an oxygenated fluid she could breathe. Kipper shuddered. She loved and hated that spaceship so much.

But this spaceship—this brand new, untested spaceship—was entirely hers. It could be her home for real. This crew could become her family, the way that the Jolly Barracuders had. The way Trugger still was.

But they would have to make it through today. And today would be a crucible that would forge their bonds, forming them into an unbreakable unit... or it would break them. She didn't know which. She had collected the strongest, most well-balanced crew that she knew how to... but then Alistair had lost re-election; the golden furred menace, Champ Truman, had taken office; and everything had started going to hell.

Most of the cats in the Uplifted States didn't know yet how bad it could become. They didn't have friends still involved at the highest levels of the government, keeping them informed on the inner workings, and the changes that were coming. But while Kipper's brother and sister—Alistair and Petra—had been out on their ears as soon as the government was handed over to Champ, Trudith was the kind of dog who could get along with anyone—even First Racer idiots out to glue cats' paws to the ground forever, because they believed humans had given dogs the godly right to rule over their feline neighbors.

But even if Trudith *could* get along with those kinds of crazy dogs, she was still deeply loyal in her heart to Kipper and Alistair. So, she passed along any information she was included on —because she was the kind of dog that those in power liked to have around, but then forgot she was still there and listening when they started discussing their indiscretions—as discretely as possible to her adopted cat family. Because like Trugger, Trudith was family.

Another dog who had gracefully survived the handover of the government from Alistair to Champ was Vice President Morrison. Oh yes, the moment he'd had a chance to hitch his wagon to one pulled by a dog instead of a cat, Morrison had abandoned the politically-expedient alliance with Alistair and run for Vice President again, but on Champ's ticket.

And Morrison had convinced Champ to bring back his bill to

ban cats from space. Just what all the cats of the Uplifted States had needed—a scheming Sheltie pulling the puppet strings on an affable, easy-to-like Golden Retriever.

So, Kipper wasn't just fighting to save her space program. She was fighting to save the rights of all the cats in the Uplifted States.

And today would be critical in that fight. So, she sighed long and hard when the final dawn-touched cloud melted into a glaringly blue sky.

She was going to break through that sky with her spaceship, and she was going to make damn sure that the crack she broke into it stayed wide open for her niece, nephews, and every other kitten growing up with dreams of someday joining all the otters who lived in the space stations scattered throughout the sky.

The rest of the crew finally began filtering onto the bridge from their restless nights of anticipation. The four mice had shining eyes, full of hope and excitement. Kipper suspected that Trugger had let something slip to them, and they had guesses about what was coming.

The cats, Hedda and Katasha, were all business, checking the readouts on the ship's dormant engines. Engineers to the core, they only had eyes for the ship. The dogs, Freddy and Georgie, were talking rapidly to each other in MSL, paws moving in beautiful, intricate dances. Kipper didn't know MSL as well as she knew Swimmer's Sign, but she knew enough to pick up that the brothers were talking about their family, and how excited they'd all be watching the launch.

The new dog, Amelia, and the squirrel, Sequoia, were much more sedate than all the others. That didn't surprise Kipper. Amelia had been assigned to this crew after the fact, and Sequoia was supposed to be the ship's navigator. If they were only taking a short jaunt to the moon and back today, then her skills wouldn't be called into play. She probably felt like a fifth wheel. Well, that would change soon enough.

Trugger and Obsidian came onto the bridge last, the octopus perched on the river otter's shoulders, waving his tentacles around mock-menacingly. "I'm a velociraptor!" Trugger said, holding his paws in front of him, curled downward, in a silly imitation of a velociraptor's talons.

"And I'm an octopus!" Obsidian signed. Together, the two of them seemed to be pretending to be a bonded octopus-raptor pair.

Kipper quirked a smile. Though, she probably shouldn't encourage them. Still, it was interesting watching the rest of the room's response—the mice tittered nervously; Sequoia smiled; Hedda rolled her eyes, and Katasha barely looked up from the engine readings. Both dachshund brothers guffawed, and Amelia frowned, an expression almost hidden by the fringe of curls around her muzzle. Though, Kipper noticed that the curly-furred dog had braided the hair around her eyes, giving her a clearer view. That was a smart move. Long fur could be hard to manage in zero gee.

"Okay," Kipper said. "Just to be clear here, even though Earth just underwent a war with the velociraptors who used to rule Jupiter, they've been overthrown by the octopuses they'd been enslaving. The entire Jovian society of octopuses and velociraptors is in complete upheaval, and many velociraptors have defected, becoming essentially our allies. Including our crew member, Gy'krr, who has yet to join us."

"Right," Trugger agreed. "So, when Gy'krr and Nioli get here..."

"*When?*" Sequoia snorted, and Kipper thought she was probably hearing some of the bitterness that the squirrel might feel about the extremely limited nature of today's mission. Today's *official* mission. "I've been brushing up on Uplifted States politics, and you're never gonna get clearance to have a bonded octopus-raptor pair join our crew." The squirrel's expression was grim.

"Actually," Kipper said, smiling beneficently at the curly-furred mop dog who suddenly looked very uncomfortable. "We already have the clearance, thanks to Amelia."

"A lot of good it'll do," Sequoia muttered, "if we're never authorized to fly as far as Europa."

Trugger caught Kipper's eye, and the two of them kept the best poker faces they could manage.

"Sorry," Sequoia said, "I just..."

"You saw the news article this morning about Vice President Morrison's speech." Kipper hadn't watched the video of the speech herself. She couldn't stand that smug Sheltie's muzzle. But Trudith had leaked the planned text of the speech to her ahead of time, so she'd known what to expect.

"Yeah," Sequoia agreed. "And if you read between the lines..."

"Yes, clearly, he's bucking for making our first mission our last mission, but Trugger and I have known this was coming for some time. And we're not going to give up the USSA that easily."

Everyone on the bridge was watching Kipper now, and she felt the weight of their gaze fall heavily on her—their hopes, expectations, and fear of disappointment if they dared to feel those hopes too keenly. She understood better how ridiculous Captain Cod could be now that she had taken on his role as leader of a spaceship crew—it was a lot to carry, and a little levity probably made those weights fall more lightly on the shoulders.

And yet, she couldn't bring herself to break the tension with a joke or metaphor about birds.

Today was too important.

Kipper spoke solemnly, seriously, and completely sincerely, signing along with her paws in Swimmer's Sign: "Whatever comes next for the USSA will depend on how our mission goes today, so let's show the world that the Uplifted States Space

Administration has the best spaceship in the whole solar system. Let's show them what *The Lucky Boomerang* can do."

Smiles broke across muzzles of varying sizes throughout the room. Even Obsidian blushed a lovely shade of sunset pink.

But most importantly, Amelia didn't seem to suspect a thing. Because of her presence, Kipper couldn't afford to bring anyone into her confidences until they were in the extranational waters of deep space. She couldn't tell anyone what she really had planned. Except Trugger, of course.

"Let's all get to our stations and get this launch underway," Trugger said and signed, dismissing everyone to begin their day's work. Obsidian slithered his way down from Trugger's shoulders, and then the otter came over to put a paw reassuringly on Kipper's shoulder. "We've got this," he said.

Kipper nodded, trying to buck up her own spirits, internally, the way she had done for everyone else. The unwavering smile on Trugger's face helped.

And then the smile faded, and Trugger turned deeply serious. He leaned close to her and said in a low voice, "But I do have to correct one thing you said."

"What?" Kipper asked, genuinely concerned.

"*The Lucky Boomerang* may be the fastest ship in the entire solar system, with its epsilon drive... but *The Jolly Barracuda* is still the *best*."

Kipper sighed deeply. But she knew better than to argue. Trugger's loyalty was one of his best traits, and she would never succeed in arguing him out of it. She wouldn't want to.

The crew scurried around the ship, getting every last detail ready for their launch. Kipper felt strange and useless in her captain's chair—in the middle of it all, and yet, somehow not entirely a part of it.

That's how Kipper felt about the world too. She'd watched the political scene grow more and more divided during the course of her brother's presidency... It wasn't his fault. He was the first feline president, and it was inevitable that a cat ascending to the highest position in the country would draw out all the crackpot, nutjob, diehard First Racer dogs who wanted to hold cats down, no matter how good of a president he'd turned out to be.

But knowing it was inevitable, and knowing that overall the country was making progress, in spite of the setbacks being thrown at them by Champ Truman... it didn't make her feel any better. She felt like she was drowning on Earth; and she felt like she was only a visitor in the otter society in the sky. She hoped this spaceship and the USSA would change that. She was about to be back in the sky—the beautiful, wonderful, infinite sky— but this time she'd be there on her own terms, not hitching a lift from a generous otter.

Of course, how long that would last all depended on how well she'd understood the composition of her crew. Because a spaceship isn't worth much without a crew to fly it.

She'd find out soon enough. As soon as *The Lucky Boomerang* was settled into a safe orbit, just past the dark side of the moon, it would be time for the whole crew to have a very serious conversation.

Pushing the anticipation—both hope and fear—of that conversation aside, Kipper let the ritual, details, and structure of the launch flow past her. Her only job was to keep track of all those details, making sure that each necessary step was taken before the crew moved onto the next.

Once the ship was ready—engines humming—and the government dogs in the air control tower gave them the green light to launch, every member of the crew pulled their jumpsuit spacesuits over their uniforms. There shouldn't be any need for them, but you don't launch a prototype vessel into space without being ready for something to go wrong, so they all needed to suit up.

The uniforms were made from a new kind of fabric—the

formula for it was yet another one of the invaluable discoveries that Jenny and her team on Europa had extracted and translated from the treasure trove of ancient octopus computers, along with the plans for the epsilon drive itself and also faster-than-light communications arrays.

"Okay," Trugger said, wiggling his long spine as he shimmied into the new spacesuit. "I have to grant—these suits are better than anything we had on *The Jolly Barracuda*." He zipped the suit up the front, and the fabric shimmered like the rainbowy surface of a bubble. He flipped the spacesuit's hood over his head, snapped the attached faceplate into its rigid form and sealed the edges of the hood around it.

The whole suit looked as clear as the surface of a very deep lake, catching reflections and obscuring them strangely with every slight movement.

Kipper pulled her own spacesuit hood over her head, snapped the faceplate in place, and broke into a huge grin. "It feels like... nothing," she said.

"A bit of an improvement over that otter suit you had to wear way back when, eh?" Trugger grinned back.

Kipper's ears flattened at the mere memory of how that spacesuit helmet with its space for tiny, round otter ears had crushed her own triangular ears down. She shuddered all the way down to the twitchy tip of her tail, which as usual with a spacesuit was pressed against her leg inside the pant leg. But still, she wasn't saddled with a big old baggy, empty sack for an otter's rudder tail flapping around uselessly behind her. "Yeah, I'd say this is better."

The rest of the crew looked happy with their spacesuits too, even Obsidian who could still communicate via the color of his skin through the transparent fabric wrapped around his tentacles.

Once everyone was in place, properly suited, Kipper gave the order, and the engines roared to life.

"The epsilon drive will be a lot quieter than that," Katasha said. "These are just the booster engines for escaping Earth's atmosphere." The tabby-point Siamese cat's post was on the bridge, but she was monitoring the engines and staying in communication with Hedda, the calico cat running the engine room.

The mice and dachshund brothers were down in the engine room too, working with Hedda. Whereas Obsidian, Sequoia, Trugger, and now Amelia all had posts on the bridge, arranged at computer stations all around Kipper. Fortunately, there had been enough room on the bridge to accommodate an extra, unwanted government dog, added to the crew at the last minute.

"To the stars!" Kipper said, slicing her paw through the air in a way that made it clear it was time for Katasha to engage the booster engines.

"Well, at least, the moon," Sequoia quipped, still seemingly bitter about the limited nature of their mission.

Kipper shot the squirrel an unamused expression that quieted her down instantly. Trugger decided to help by saying, "And after all, isn't the moon really a kind of star? The biggest and brightest one in the Earth's sky?"

Every animal on the bridge turned to stare at Trugger, but the otter felt no shame over the ridiculousness of his statement. "Hey, at least I didn't compare the moon to an ostrich egg, lost on the waving dunes of a black sand desert."

"I think that would've been better," Kipper said.

"It certainly wouldn't have been any less factual," Sequoia agreed.

And Trugger quirked a smile at Kipper—his ridiculous statement had put her and the unhappy squirrel on the same side, defending reality from the encroaching silliness of otters. And that had clearly been his plan.

Crew interactions aside, it was time to launch.

How do you describe a spaceship launch?

From the ground, watching it, the ship streaks through the sky, piercing higher and higher into the thick blue like a needle cutting through a layer of fabric that protects our world from the emptiness outside. White smoke trails after the ship like a cottony strand of thread, hanging from the needle.

Inside the ship, it's like being strapped into the car of a rollercoaster—everything rumbles, everything quivers and shakes, and your stomach falls and flips, no matter how much you've trained, no matter how much you're prepared, because mammalian stomachs didn't evolve for that kind of travel. Our bodies never expected to leave this world, even as our minds yearned for escape and adventure.

But all of that is wrong. Too simplistic.

The most important part is that the world falls away, as if gravity had never really been a law, as if it's something you can forget, and when you forget, the bonds tying you to the planet you were born on, grew up on, lived on and walked on... become nothing. You are meant for the sky.

And the world that had been your whole world becomes so very small, you can see the whole thing at once. Every place you've been, every person you've met, every memory that you built while living on the planet all become small enough to fit inside a single sphere that fills less than the entirety of your vision. You can see more than you've ever seen before, and you can see it all at once.

Kipper's heart swelled as she watched the ground recede, horizon broadening beneath them. The clouds slipped past the viewscreen in their shades of ash gray to pearly white, filling the view until the last wisp of cloud cleared, leaving a rippled, crenulated, landscape of whipped cream beneath them and emptiness all around. But Earth still filled the viewscreen—blue oceans glowing under the smears of soft white. Eventually, the curved edges of the Earth came into view, closing the landscape into something contained.

Kipper felt herself becoming a part of the wider society filling her homeworld's solar system once again. On Earth, it's easy to think that Earth is everything, and everything beyond Earth is small. But when you're in the sky, your entire perspective flips, and the place that held you becomes a something you can hold in your vision, in your mind. The cradle becomes the thing that needs cradling.

Just a sphere of blue, white, and touches of green. Just an eye, staring back at you, holding your gaze as steadily as you can stare back.

On the Earth, when you blink, you can still feel the planet all around you. The air, the gravity, the sounds. It holds you, whispers to you, and fills your lungs. You can't imagine it could disappear, not really. But in space, blink for a split second, and for that moment, the whole world could be gone. You can't feel its hold on you anymore, except maybe in your heart.

Kipper had seen beautiful sights in her travels—the creamsicle clouds of Jupiter, the ice fields of Europa, and the octopus city of Choir's Deep, bursting with all the colors of underwater life. But the sight of Earth, curled up and small, like a child sleeping, was still one of the most beautiful sights she'd ever seen. It always would be. It had all the majesty of space... and all the comfort and familiarity of gazing at your mother's face.

"Geosynchronous orbit achieved," Katasha said, floating at her station now, only held in place by a seatbelt, as they all were. They'd left gravity behind, along with all the rules and control of the dog-run government. "Booster engines have powered down, and the epsilon drive is ready for its first test on your command, Captain Kipper."

"Let's get right to it then," Kipper said. "Begin the epsilon drive jump to the far side of the moon at will."

Katasha didn't hesitate. She was a young engineer, scooped straight out of college and drafted into the new USSA program for her brilliant, cutting edge designs. That eagerness combined with her gray tabby stripes—even if they were only a mask on her face and gloves on her paws, due to her Siamese heritage—made Kipper feel like she was looking into a distorted mirror on her past whenever she watched Katasha. This young cat was who she could have been, if she'd been born a few years later, young enough to see a feline president before understanding the weight of history that had had to be lifted to raise him to that position, and had been raised herself in a family instead of a cattery, taught to value herself instead of doubt herself.

Kipper felt proud and, honestly, a little threatened by Katasha. She wished she could have been a cat like her, instead of one of the cats who'd had to pave the way for her.

Suddenly, every thought in Kipper's mind was cut off by the sensation of jumping through space. The feeling completely enveloped Kipper before she'd had time to brace against it: cold and hot, bright and dark, pleasurable and painful, all at once. It was as if every nerve and every neuron in her body sparked at the same time—fire and ice, whisper and shout, dream and unmistakable reality, blended into an impossible mix.

And then it was over, as fast it had begun, and Kipper found herself staring at the far side of the moon. The silver sphere wasn't dark. It was the wrong time of the month for that; the sun shone steadily on the unfamiliar, pockmarked, ashy gray surface. This was the moon's other face, and it would watch over her ship, as her crew decided whether they would accompany her on her planned, rogue mission.

"Trugger," Kipper said, "send a message back to Earth saying that the jump was a success, but that we'll be going silent for a while as we double and triple check all of our systems, just to be sure."

"What?" Katasha objected. "We don't need to—"

"Everyone else," Kipper said, ignoring the outburst from her younger mirror, "follow me to the galley. We have a change of plans to discuss. Trugger will run the ship while we do. Please pass that information along to everyone in engineering, Katasha."

The Siamese-tabby dipped her ears and nodded deferentially, looking both non-plussed and intrigued. Kipper supposed that was a fair reaction. The young engineer was one of the officers for whom Kipper was least sure of what to expect in the coming conversation. Youth is inherently unpredictable. Furthermore, citizens of the Uplifted States had more to lose by going rogue on this mission.

Kipper was about to ask her crew to assist her in stealing a spaceship.

CHAPTER 9
SEQUOIA

The last twelve hours of Sequoia's life had been an absolute rollercoaster of emotions. She'd learned during her months with the USSA that among the dogs of the Uplifted States, squirrels were stereotyped as flighty, impulsive, mercurial creatures, ruled by emotions as unpredictable as ocean waves during a storm. That was nothing like how Sequoia had always seen herself. She knew herself, and she'd always considered herself to be steady, steadfast, and certain. As fixed as the distant stars in the sky which she treasured so much.

But these last few hours had rocked her heart like a small boat on that metaphorical ocean of emotions.

Perhaps, the day before *The Lucky Boomerang's* first flight hadn't been the best time to start researching Uplifted States politics, but in fairness to herself and that decision, she could never have expected to discover such a tangled web of religion-induced ignorance and xenophobic speciesism.

She'd known that the dogs (other than Freddy and Georgie in the engine room) who she'd encountered since joining the crew had behaved very strangely around her. She hadn't realized that they saw her entire species—as well as mice and otters—as completely irrelevant, long since discarded stepping stones on the ladder of Uplift. As far as First Racer dogs were concerned, only dogs (and maybe cats, if they were well-behaved enough) mattered at all. Everyone else was, at best, unnecessary and, more likely, a dangerous distraction when it came to their important work of... waiting.

Yes, they were supposed to be waiting for humans to return from the stars, and that just seemed insane. Sure, the history records were clear that some humans had escaped Earth before the plague that killed the remaining ones, but why would they come back? They'd been travelling to populate the stars. Earth was nothing to whatever humans might have survived those interstellar travels. Nothing but a shell they'd discarded, leaving it for the uplifted animals.

Sequoia wouldn't care about what all the dogs of the Uplifted States believed, but those dogs were bankrolling this space program.

Also... she'd started looking into dog beliefs, because she kinda had a crush on Amelia. It was dumb, but that scruffy dog's tail had started wagging so hard at the final press conference when Kipper talked about how *The Lucky Boomerang* might uncover evidence of where humans had traveled to among the stars. And dang, but Amelia was just so cute when her tail wagged like that, and her face totally covered in tawny curls? Adorable.

Sequoia's heart had started to go pitter-pat in the kind of way that was probably what caused all the dogs she kept meeting to bark at her about her tail being too distracting. She didn't like understanding or sympathizing with that kind of bad behavior at all. But... also, she could not get the image of Amelia's curl-obscured smile out of her mind, and the rhythm of the mop-dog's wagging tail felt like it danced in step with the beating of her squirrel heart.

It was just a crush. It would go away.

In fact, it was probably caused by her nerves about today's flight, which had been a whole emotional rollercoaster of its own. Her brain felt like a whole amusement park full of heart-stopping rides, whooshing about and full of screaming, right now.

Because, of course, researching First Racer beliefs had led Sequoia to discover what Kipper had been trying to distract them all from—the USSA was going to be cancelled by President Champ Truman. There would be no interstellar travels; *The Lucky Boomerang* would take one lap around the moon, and then be retired unceremoniously. Back to Treesylvania for her and Mousfordshire for the mice. All of it for nothing. No stars to hold in her paws.

But then... she'd heard the mice giggling together, and she wasn't sure, but they seemed to think they knew something. Something secret. Something Trugger had let slip...

And so hope and disappointment warred in Sequoia's heart, right alongside the war between her crush on Amelia and fury at her for representing everything bad about Uplifted States, First Racer dogs.

With all those feelings roiling inside her, Sequoia sedately floated along after Kipper, drifting weightlessly through the halls of *The Lucky Boomerang* toward the galley. She was painfully aware of Amelia floating along behind her, and she kept her bushy tail as still as possible because of it. She didn't know if Amelia had understood that braiding her fur had been a way to flirt with her, and she wasn't sure that she wanted the dog to figure it out. She'd hoped that braiding Amelia's curls would get the crush out of her system... but those curls had been so silky, and the brown eyes underneath so full of adorable bewilderment.

Among squirrels, in Treesylvania where she'd grown up, a flitting tail might betray something of its owner's feelings, but in and of itself would never be interpreted as flirting. Sequoia wasn't used to controlling the manic twitching of her tail like she'd had to learn how to do since joining the USSA. She didn't like it. She wanted to just be herself and let her tail wave frenetically, expressing all the complicated twitchy feelings in her heart.

When they arrived at the galley—a room at the top of the ship, with windows looking out at the stars all around them—Kipper took a seat at the head of the long galley table. The tabby cat moved with a grace in the zero gravity environment that look practiced, carefully earned by hours spent in space among the otters of her old crew. The younger cat, Katasha, bumped her way along much more awkwardly, bouncing between floor and ceiling, until she settled into the seat beside Captain Kipper. Each cat hooked their hind paws into the stools rooted to the galley's floor so they wouldn't float away.

Sequoia chose a seat further down. Her heart pounded when Amelia chose the seat beside her. What did that mean? Why did she care? Sequoia was in space, for the first time, closer to the stars she loved than she'd ever been before, and yet her heart was distracted by the presence of a ridiculous mop-dog who probably thought of her as less than a full person.

The octopus, Obsidian, streamed into the room like his tentacles were more liquid than solid. He looked larger than Sequoia had ever seen him before, stretching out his tentacles to take up all the space available to him, instead of squished down by gravity, pressing him against the floor. He settled on the ceiling, which was just another wall, albeit window-filled, now that they were in zero gee. Though, it was a wall above the rest of their heads, and his tentacles blocked out the stars like an extremely strange cloud formation. His colors fluctuated, fluttering through the spectrum of every shade. He was a living rainbow or perhaps an aurora borealis, and Sequoia would have thought for sure that he would be the most mesmerizing member of the crew to stare at during the meeting... but then the mice came tumbling into the room, showing off every acrobatic skill they had among them.

Only three of the four mice were former gymnasts, but the fourth one must have picked up a few moves hanging out with them, because all four of them flipped and twirled through the air like an entire miniature circus, their tails chasing after them like streamers.

Hedda, Freddy, and Georgie followed the mice, and all of them settled around the table. The mice had their own miniature table and stools built onto the surface of the end of the table, so they could sit at a comparable height to everyone else. Not that heights mattered so much, now that they were in space and the gravity was gone. But as Sequoia understood it, the otters studying the ancient octopus base on Europa were still hoping to uncover schematics for an artificial gravity generator, and *The Lucky Boomerang* had been built with those hopes in mind.

And it would be retired with those hopes turned to ash, trodden under the paws of a lot of religious dogs.

And Sequoia wouldn't get to see the distant stars up close, massive and breathtaking, and the sun from far away, sparkling and small like all the other stars in the sky.

At the head of the table, Captain Kipper snapped the seal between her spacesuit's faceplate and the hood holding it in place. Then she lowered the hood behind her head, so it hung down behind her back with the faceplate loosely affixed to one side. She gestured for the others to follow suit if they desired.

Once the group settled down, most of them with their spacesuit hoods lowered—the notable exception being Obsidian, who seemed more comfortable in his water-filled spacesuit than he'd seemed in the dry air—the captain began to speak:

"I picked each one of you for this crew myself," Kipper said. Everyone else at the table glanced at Amelia, who had been foisted on them last minute, as she said this. But the captain's gaze didn't flicker, didn't favor anyone over anyone else. She stared down the table, taking them all in evenly. "I believe in and respect every one of you, and that's why you all need to be included in this conversation."

"What about Trugger?" Katasha asked. The otter was the only crewmember still on the bridge.

"He's my right-hand otter," Kipper said. "He and I have already discussed the coming mission, and I know where he stands. But I want to give each one of you a chance to make your own choice."

Hope danced in Sequoia's heart at the idea of a choice.

If Kipper was offering them a choice...

Maybe today's mission wasn't over just yet.

"What choice?" Hedda asked. The calico cat engineer's gold eyes gleamed with curiosity.

"In spite of our tireless work to get authorization for an actual deep space mission," Kipper said, "this test drive to the dark side of the moon was all we could get permission for from the current government. Obviously, that is not enough. A ship like this deserves a real test drive. A real chance to show what it —and its crew—are capable of."

The variegated crew of animals around the table grew very quiet, waiting to hear the exact choice Kipper would offer them. Sequoia could hear her own heart racing in the silence. She noticed a flash in Amelia's eyes, as the dog sat beside her. Was it anger? The dog's pose had grown stiff, like she was bracing for a fight—she'd leaned back, while everyone else had leaned forward, eager and intrigued. Hopeful.

"Trugger and I plan to continue our mission, in spite of the government's refusal to back us up. We won't let *The Lucky Boomerang* be mothballed just because we weren't willing to take a risk and prove its value." Kipper drew a deep breath, lowered her head, and stared levelly at the whole group. "We plan to fly to Europa and pick up our remaining crewmembers—Nioli and

Gy'krr the bonded octopus and raptor pair. From there, we intend to explore deep space, searching for signs or traces of extrasolar civilizations, possibly even human colonies on other worlds."

If silence can become more silent, the silence in *The Lucky Boomerang's* galley did so.

"Technically," Kipper said, "this means we'll be stealing this spaceship. If we do find anything of value out among the stars... that indiscretion will likely be forgiven by the Uplifted States government. Ask for forgiveness, not permission, right? But if we don't find anything of value..." Kipper shrugged. "Well, I can handle living the rest of my life as a political refugee. There are plenty of great places to live in our solar system outside of the Uplifted States, and I know my sister and brother would come visit me. But I don't want to inflict that kind of exile on any of you."

An uncomfortable rustling diminished the silence as the different members of the crew shuffled in their seats, looking from one neighbor to the next, trying to figure out how their crewmates would choose.

"So this is your chance," Kipper said, "if any of you don't want to risk your future in the Uplifted States, gambling it on this mission, then I've arranged for *The Jolly Barracuda*, my previous ship, to rendezvous with us and offer safe passage back to Earth to you now."

"This is ridiculous!" The curly-furred mop dog was shaking with fury after her outburst. Amelia's eyes smoldered, framed by the pretty braids that revealed them to onlookers. The way her gaze darted from one crewmember to the next suggested she was trying to gauge whether they'd follow her in a mutiny and hoping to intimidate them into believing they no choice but to help her overthrow Captain Kipper. She also brushed her paw against the side of her face in a way that made Sequoia think it hadn't been a mistake that she'd kept her eyes hidden before—

this dog didn't like other people being able to look her in the eye.

Sequoia found that kind of endearing—Amelia might put up a bold front, but it was just that: a front. She was masking, trying to hide the uncertainty she felt inside.

Sequoia raised her paw and said, "As far as I can tell, half of the dogs in the Uplifted States already think I'm a criminal just for being a squirrel. I have no problem with adding spaceship theft to my rap sheet. I would follow you to the farthest star, Captain Kipper. Especially because I've wanted to travel to the stars for as long as I can remember anyway. Count me in."

If Amelia looked angry before, she was seething now.

One by one, the mice chimed in to agree—there was no life for them in the Uplifted States anyway, and they'd already planned to return to Mousfordshire after their time with the USSA ended.

Obsidian signed his answer with tentacle tips blushed as gleaming black as his name. He would follow Captain Kipper too.

That left only crewmembers who actually were dogs and cats of the Uplifted States. Freddy and George had turned toward each other and were both signing rapidly, holding their paws low and close, obscured enough by their shoulders and the edge of the table that no one else could quite make out what they were signing to each other.

Katasha's dark ears had flattened, and her clear blue eyes looked troubled. Hedda had only lowered one of her ears, giving her splotchy Halloween-colored, calico face a skewed expression; her golden eyes had gone all distant and dreamy. She was the first to speak: "Captain, do you have any reason to expect that you *will* find something valuable on this mission?"

"Exploration of our galaxy is intrinsically valuable," Sequoia quipped. Though, she knew she probably shouldn't have. It wasn't what Hedda had meant, and it was true that it wouldn't buy the calico cat a way home after stealing a multi-million dollar, government-funded spaceship. But the squirrel just couldn't resist, largely because it made Amelia bristle even more. That adorable, scruffy mop was just this side of actually growling.

"If you're asking whether I have privileged information that leads me to believe our mission will be a success..." Captain Kipper's ears dipped, in spite of the fact that she was clearly struggling to keep them standing tall. "No, I don't know anything that you don't. There hasn't been some secret discovery in the ancient octopus archives on Europa. I'm gambling with my life here, and if I lose the gamble, I'll only get to see my niece and two nephews when my sister brings them to visit me outside of the Uplifted States for the rest of my life."

Freddy and Georgie stopped signing to each other to watch Kipper's paws as she mirrored her spoken words with signs.

"So... yes, I do really believe that it's a worthwhile gamble. But no, I don't know anything that the rest of you don't. We may simply visit a few stars, gather a little astrophysical and astronomical data, and come back with nothing that the politicians who could retroactively excuse our little jaunt would care about."

All of the cats' ears had flattened by this point.

"But... you think we could find positions among the otter space fleet?" Hedda's voice had grown high and querulous. This was clearly a stressful choice for the animals who actually lived and had families in the Uplifted States.

"I can't make any guarantees," Kipper said, "but anyone who stays aboard *The Lucky Boomerang* for this coming mission will be among the first crew of interstellar travelers in our entire solar system."

"Except for the First Race," Amelia grumbled. She'd leaned way back, arms crossed protectively across her chest. She seemed to have checked out emotionally from the proceedings.

Sequoia supposed her crush on the dog would stop being a problem when Amelia opted out of the mission. Out of sight, out of mind. Then the squirrel could go back to focusing on her beloved stars—stars that she was about to get a whole lot closer to. Her heart raced with excitement.

At some level, Sequoia didn't care what the cats and dogs of the engine room chose to do... as long as there were enough engineers left for them to run the ship.

"Being one of the first interstellar travelers in the solar system seems like it would *have* to count for something when looking for a new position on a spaceship," Yvette squeaked. The gray mouse was holding her tail in her paws, twisting it nervously. The mice had been more closely involved in working on *The Lucky Boomerang's* engines than Sequoia, and suddenly the squirrel realized that maybe she should be worried about what would happen if all four of the engine dogs and cats defected here...

"More than that," Sequoia chimed in, "if *The Lucky Boomerang* gets mothballed and the USSA cancelled, there *won't be any space-ships* associated with the Uplifted States. So, if you want to keep working on spaceship engines, the otters will be your only option. Might as well impress them while you have the chance. Everyone aboard *The Lucky Boomerang* will be solar system experts on interstellar travel after this mission, no matter what we discover."

Captain Kipper pointed a carefully extended claw toward Sequoia, showing she agreed with the squirrel's point. In response, Sequoia's spacesuit-sheathed tail flipped and twitched behind her. Deep down, the squirrel enjoyed praise as much as any dog. Especially when it came from someone she respected as much as Captain Kipper—the Hero of Europa.

George glanced nervously at his brother, and the skinnier dachshund looked away huffily. George looked back at the captain and signed, "We're in. My brother is worried about how our mother will take the news, but he knows we need to do this."

"Is that right?" Kipper asked, pinning Freddy with a questioning look.

The skinny dachshund nodded, once quickly. He didn't expand on what his brother had said for him.

Katasha drew a deep breath and said, "That's what I'm worried about—how my boyfriend will take the news. I wish I could have warned him. Instead..."

"He'll hear it on the news, not from you," Kipper said, completing the thought. "I know. I'm sorry about that. But if the slightest whisper of our plans had gotten out ahead of time..."

"You'd have been thrown in jail, and President Truman would have thrown away the key," Amelia grumbled. "You're committing sedition right now. And if it goes the way it looks like it's going, you'll all be committing treason."

That's when Trugger burst into the room, gliding like an arrow, and said, "Treason, like a parrot's tears, is in the eye of the beholder."

"Are the tears... not in the parrot's eyes?" Katasha asked.

"Do parrots even cry?" Yvette squeaked.

Kipper just sighed. She'd clearly known Trugger the longest. She was used to him.

"Parakeets cry when feathers line the passage of time." Trugger said, becoming even more arcane. He whipped himself around in a curlicue, ending up floating above the table, between all the mammals seated at it and Obsidian still clinging to the windowed ceiling with his sucker disks.

"You've switched from parrots to parakeets," Katasha irritably observed, ears skewing in a complicated dance. "You know they're different right?"

"The important thing," Trugger said, "is that *The Jolly Barracuda* is ready to rendezvous with us, and USSA control is getting increasingly frantic about recalling us to Earth. Has everyone decided what they're doing?"

"Not yet," Kipper said.

Sequoia stared across the table at the two cats who were still undecided. Could the mission continue safely without them? Freddy and Georgie both worked in the engine room, but Hedda was the chief engineer. And Katasha seemed to be some kind of wunderkind, plucked straight out of college (before she'd even graduated) to join the crew.

Captain Kipper wasn't revealing a lot with her stoic expression, but Sequoia suspected the mission would be in serious trouble without Hedda and Katasha. There weren't a lot of extra hands aboard this ship. Every one of them was needed.

But maybe Captain Kipper and Trugger had backup plans? Maybe they knew otters who could fill Hedda and Katasha's places?

Or maybe the whole mission would end up stuck in the bureaucratic hell of negotiating for otters to join the crew, waiting and treading water until the whole thing went under and stealing a spaceship from the Uplifted States government turned out to be for nothing.

Would any otters want to touch this rebel mission?

Or would that be construed as an act of war by this wretched President Champ Truman and his administration of rabid First Racers?

Sequoia needed to say something. She needed to say something inspiring. Something that would motivate these reluctant cats to get onboard, because she couldn't come this close to touching the stars and have it all fall apart here.

"What's holding you back?" Sequoia chittered. "Because I've been in your country for only a few months, mostly cloistered on this spaceship, and even I can see how badly cats get treated in the Uplifted States. Why do you care about going back to that?"

"Because it's my home," Hedda said glumly. The calico cat's splotchy ears weren't so much flattened now as simply sagging.

"Also," Katasha pointed out, "Freddy and Georgie might be able to cut some kind of deal and come back. If we do this? That's it for going home. You said that you can see how badly cats get treated? Well, it gets even worse if you've ever stepped out of line, even the smallest amount. We have to be perfect."

Sequoia's voice got low and sympathetic, "It doesn't have to be like that."

"And it's not like that everywhere," Kipper said.

"What should I tell USSA control?" Trugger asked. "Is the mission on?"

Kipper's eyes widened, and her lips drew back in a grimace revealing her sharp fangs. Clearly, Trugger had revealed more than she wanted him to.

And Sequoia was right.

This whole mission hinged on getting everyone to opt into it. Or least, more than had agreed to follow Kipper so far.

"Tell them we're coming home," Amelia said. "We had a little engine trouble, nothing serious, and we'll be returning shortly." The mop dog let her braid-framed eyes pass from one member of the crew to the next, lingering the longest on Captain Kipper. "Take this deal now, and I'll tell no one about this conversation."

Sequoia's heart sank. That was it. She looked up at the windowed ceiling, and it felt like the stars, framed by the curlicues of Obsidian's purple-gray tentacles, were receding farther and farther away from her. Always out of grasp.

"No," Katasha said, growling at Amelia, "it's First Racer dogs like you and Champ Truman who sold my boyfriend's family a cult about how they're not only less good than dogs because they're cats, but they're also less good than other cats because they're not part of some weird purebred line that humans set up before disappearing. He's spent years recovering from that nonsense. And if we can find anything in the stars to help debunk your whole damned awful religion, then I want to be part of that, and he'll understand." Katasha's triangular ears stood tall as she turned her clear blue eyes toward Captain Kipper. "Count me in."

Suddenly, Kipper looked a whole lot more comfortable. "Alright then, Trugger, keep stalling with USSA control, but it looks like we'll need *The Jolly Barracuda* to pick up Hedda and Amelia?" The captain's voice rose, making it clear she was still asking. It still wasn't too late to join her.

Hedda's gold eyes looked troubled, but she said, "I'll come. The Uplifted States might be my home, but Katasha's right. This is a chance to make my home better... even if I lose it for myself in the process." The calico cat got up from her seat and floated past Trugger toward the corridor she'd entered through. "I'm going back to my engine room now."

Captain Kipper nodded and said, "The rest of you may return to your posts as well. Except for Trugger and Amelia. The two of you hold back for a minute. But the rest of you, prepare for a very exciting mission!"

Sequoia's heart felt like the rollercoaster it had been riding had just pulled up to the top of the biggest, steepest hill, and oh goodness, was she ready for the loop-de-looping dive to come! This was gonna be the thrill of a lifetime.

A huge grin spread across the squirrel's small muzzle, and she waved her paw tauntingly at the frowning mop dog as she floated away. "Buh-bye, Amelia. I hope you liked the braids, but I guess you won't be needing them much longer." She made a point of flipping her bushy red tail as she sailed out of the room, letting it flap and flutter like a flag in a heavy wind.

That curly-furred dog could eat her heart out. She wouldn't be troubling Sequoia's heart any more. Sequoia's heart had stars to love.

CHAPTER 10
KIPPER

"I'm staying," Amelia said.

Kipper and Trugger looked at each other, uncertain. The two of them and Amelia were the only ones left in the galley now. It wouldn't be easy to remove a stubborn dog—even a small one—from *The Lucky Boomerang* if she didn't want to go. If she wouldn't go peaceably.

Several of the other crewmembers had already shown their reluctance to break Uplifted States law and continue on the mission as Kipper planned it. It would be very, very bad for morale if those officers had to hear and see a government dog kicking and screaming as Trugger and Obsidian wrestled her out the airlock.

Though, a small part of Kipper did enjoy the idea of watching an octopus wrestle Amelia off of her ship. That dog had never belonged here in the first place. And you *do not* want to wrestle an octopus. They're all muscle.

And Obsidian would have no problem doing it. He didn't care about Uplifted States laws one bit.

Still, it would be better to avoid that outcome, amusing though it might be.

"Okay..." Kipper said cautiously, feeling her way forward.

"Why? Why do you want to stay? You clearly disagree with everything about my plans."

"Not everything," Amelia admitted. She cast her eyes downward, shifty and nervous, and one of her paws moved reflexively to touch the tiny, pretty braids around them. She looked like she wanted to tear the braids out and shield her eyes from view again.

"What part do you agree with?" Trugger asked.

"I'd rather not say," Amelia snapped, eyes narrowing into a glare that would've pierced Trugger through like a spear if he were at all bothered by dogs glaring at him.

Trugger was not.

"I can't keep you here if you're going to spend all your time trying to sabotage my position as captain, turn the crew against me, or otherwise undermine the mission," Kipper said.

Amelia shook her head. "I couldn't turn this crew against you, clearly. You're the Hero of Europa to them, and they'll follow you into the depths of outer space." The curly-furred dog shrugged. "I won't cause trouble. I just... I have a post here. It's my job to keep an eye on all of you. It's my job to monitor this mission, even if I'm monitoring how it goes *horribly wrong*. And I won't abandon my post."

Kipper's eyes narrowed as well, but not into a glare. She was thinking. Quickly, because they needed to get moving before any of the rest of the crew started to have further doubts or the Uplifted States located a sympathetic otter vessel willing to try to tow them home in return for a big payout.

"You don't think you'll be held accountable like the rest of us," Kipper said.

"I know I won't," Amelia replied. "My loyalty to the Uplifted States is not in question, and they'll understand that I had no choice given the situation up here. I'm an unwilling passenger aboard a mutinous vessel."

"Not entirely unwilling," Trugger said. "Not if you're

choosing to stay." He drew a deep sigh. "Dogs and dog governments are weird."

"Says the otter sporting green zebra stripes." Amelia frowned, as if she deeply disapproved of Trugger's decorative dye job, peeking out from the edges of his navy blue USSA uniform.

Trugger shrugged. "My weirdness only goes fur deep."

Kipper clenched her paws under the table, letting her sharp claw tips bite against her paw pads through the thin layer of her spacesuit gloves, to keep herself from laughing. Trugger was weird all the way through.

"Look, I have my reasons, and I'll be good," Amelia said, appealing to Kipper and pointedly ignoring Trugger.

"You'll be good." Kipper repeated Amelia's own words, thinking about how much goodness meant to all the dogs she'd known.

Of course, what counted as "good" could be extremely flexible.

But... She didn't want to fight Amelia.

"This is a small ship," Kipper said. "And I believe in our mission. If you get in the way—"

"You can duct tape me to the ceiling," Amelia said. "I know you have the duct tape packed."

Trugger snorted. "Of course we have duct tape. Would any sane astronaut go into space without duct tape? I don't think so."

"Duct tape would be hell on those curls," Kipper observed.

"Exactly," Amelia agreed. "I'd have to shave them all off to get the gummy gunky residue out."

"Okay, you can stay," Kipper said, wondering if she was making a huge mistake to avoid a huge inconvenience. Sometimes, neither option seems good, so you just have to pick one, and hope things get better.

And things were going to get extra-solar soon. So, probably better.

Meeting over, Kipper left the galley and floated through the halls of *The Lucky Boomerang* back toward the bridge, enjoying how on this ship, she got to swim through air instead of liquid. The halls were designed with plenty of handholds to make it easy for a cat to glide along, using her paws to guide herself. Zero gravity could be quite pleasant when it didn't come accompanied by the requirement that she drown herself in a highly oxygenated liquid atmosphere and then breathe the horrid stuff.

Running her own space program was more work than being a lackey on someone else's ship, but it did come with its advantages.

Kipper settled back into her captain's chair and then watched as the rest of the bridge crew reacted—subtly, but the reactions were there—to Amelia returning to her post. The strongest reaction came from Sequoia, the squirrel. There seemed to be some kind of tension between Sequoia and Amelia, but Kipper trusted the squirrel to behave professionally. Even if her tail had flickered like a bonfire sputtering in a gust of sea-salt wind when she saw Amelia return to her seat.

With everyone settled in their places, Kipper said, "The decision is unanimous. All of us will be proceeding with the mission as Trugger and I have planned it."

Kipper paused a moment to let the surprise in Sequoia and Katasha's eyes settle. Amelia looked away from both of them. She seemed to be a very private dog when it came to her own emotions and motivations. And Obsidian—both curled and sprawled at the same time—in his seat showed no reaction to Amelia staying whatsoever. His skin stayed the simple, dimpled red-brown that seemed to be his default, and his goat-like eyes didn't even deign to look in Amelia's direction.

Kipper nodded and drew a deep breath. She could trust her crew. Now she needed to be the captain that they trusted. And it was her responsibility to say a few words, broadcasted back to Earth. She'd practiced what she might say many times in her mind, and it was always slightly different, taking twists and turns she didn't expect. Never perfect. And she knew, whatever she said, it wouldn't only echo in her own ears forever, haunting her with how it could have been better—no, it would actually be replayed over and over again by news stations. She'd considered memorizing a short speech... but in the end, concluded that speaking a few words from the heart was more likely to go well. Even if the words weren't perfect, she'd practiced enough times to know that they would be close enough.

"Trugger, please open a channel and broadcast as widely as possible." She didn't want the USSA to disappear her words, gagging her, and letting themselves speak for the delinquent *Lucky Boomerang* crew on her behalf. As long as enough otter ships picked up the broadcast, she knew that wouldn't happen.

"Channel open... now." Trugger said, raising his paw and then lowering it suddenly on the word "now."

"Cats, dogs, and other peoples of the Uplifted States," Kipper said. "The first stage of our first homegrown space program has been a success. *The Lucky Boomerang* used its epsilon drive to jump to the far side of the moon without incident. We intend to continue our mission by jumping to Jupiter's moon Europa, and from there, we will make the first voyage from our solar system to the universe outside since..." Her voice caught a little, but that was okay. It would play well with the First Racer dogs listening. The same dogs who would be furious that she'd begun her speech by addressing "cats" before "dogs." "...ahem, the first voyage from our solar system to the outside universe since the humans who uplifted us all left the Earth."

Kipper paused, letting the momentousness of her words sink in. Not just for her listeners across the Earth and Earth's sky, but also for herself. This was a big deal.

"We don't know what we'll find outside of our solar system.

Perhaps nothing more than a few stars and empty planets on our first voyage, but what we learn on this trip could have invaluable repercussions in many scientific fields, regardless of whether we find..."

Kipper hesitated here. She had dithered back and forth for weeks about whether it would be wise or not to mention the possibility of finding humans. She wanted to raise First Racer hopes enough that they took the possibilities opened up by *The Lucky Boomerang* and its epsilon drive seriously. But she didn't want to raise them so high that her crew couldn't deliver on them. Realistically, if humans were still alive out there, and if they were easy to find... Wouldn't they have come back on their own by now?

There was no right answer. So Kipper chose one before the silence wore on too long.

"Whatever we find, it will bring us closer to knowing what the humans who uplifted us experienced when they left our solar system. We must follow in their footprints, and that means exploring the stars. Captain Kipper of *The Lucky Boomerang* out."

Kipper bowed her head when she finished speaking. Her heart was racing. She wanted to explore the universe. She wanted the freedom and thrill of flying on *The Lucky Boomerang*, farther from the Earth than any Earth-being had traveled in many lifetimes. But she didn't relish the weight of the responsibilities that came with it.

"Channel closed," Trugger said.

"I hope that was good enough," Kipper muttered before she could stop herself.

"It was beautiful," Katasha said reverently.

Kipper smiled at the compliment. Inspiring younger cats was one of her goals, and it warmed her heart to know she'd succeeded with at least one. But then she raised her eyes and turned to look at Amelia—because First Racer dogs were the demographic who would decide if she ever got to go home again after this stunt.

Amelia was trying to hide it, looking away from everyone else on the bridge, but there were tears in her eyes, wetting the delicate braids that framed them.

Good. If Kipper could move the heart of the government dog sent to keep them all on short leashes, then maybe there'd be enough positive public sentiment toward herself and the crew when they returned that their indiscretions would be forgiven. If First Racer dogs were excited enough about *The Lucky Boomerang's* mission, then President Truman would only make himself look bad by throwing a tantrum about how he'd tried and failed to stop it.

"We're receiving an incoming message from *The Jolly Barracuda,*" Trugger said with a grin big enough to melt oceans.

"Put it on the main screen," Kipper said.

A crowd of otters appeared on the screen, floating in the liquid, oxo-agua atmosphere that *The Jolly Barracuda* sported when it was prepared for flight. The big river otter in the middle of the screen—Kipper and Trugger's old captain—Captain Cod signed with his webbed paws, "Congratulations on your first epsilon drive jump, and congratulations on picking your crew so carefully that you don't need our services offloading any of them. And good luck with the rest of your mission."

"Thank you," Kipper signed back. Signing was much easier in these new spacesuits with their thin fabric than in the bulky ones she'd had to wear before now.

Captain Cod signed back, "Say 'hi' to the rest of the universe for us."

"Will do," Kipper answered with her paws before the message shut off, leaving the screen filled with the silvery curve of the moon, eclipsing the blue and green curve of Earth, all in front of a backdrop of stars.

Kipper and her crew were alone again, on the far side of the moon. An entire celestial body hung between them and the friends, family, and foes they'd left behind. And that distance was about to get a lot larger.

"Now, let's set a course for Europa—" Kipper raised her paw, waited for a nod from Katasha showing that the course was set, and concluded, "Jump at will."

They could skip putting the hoods on their spacesuits up this time. The epsilon drive had already shown it worked. Preparing for it to fail with every jump would be an overabundance of caution.

Kipper was ready for the sensation of jumping through the folds of space-time now. And yet, she also wasn't. *Would she ever be? Would it be different every time?* This time, it felt like she'd curled over—inside of and through herself—like a fiddlehead on a spring fern unfurling during a cool evening rainfall or a pre-uplift cat from the ancient times when humans still walked the Earth curling up into a tight ball on a cushion in front of a crackling fire.

When the moment ended, static still buzzed in Kipper's ears like the hissing of rain falling on leaves. The sound died away, but the change in scenery stayed: Europa filled the screen, ice blue and glass smooth. Only a small wedge of Jupiter fit into the space visible behind Europa, orange and swirly as ever.

Katasha gasped, and Sequoia made a chirping sound, halfway between laughter and a heartfelt sob. Obsidian's skin had turned the swirly shades of Jupiter's creamsicle clouds. Only Amelia—of the bridge crew members who had never traveled to Jupiter before—remained entirely composed and seemingly unmoved. She'd recovered from her reaction to Kipper's speech and seemed determined to stay stone-faced and indifferent.

Trugger grinned and said, "Jenny's calling. She has a place for us to land."

CHAPTER 11
YVETTE

The atmosphere in *The Lucky Boomerang's* engine room was riotously celebratory. The engineers didn't have the gorgeous, panoramic view of Europa that the bridge crew had been enjoying on the main viewscreen; though, smaller versions of the view were relayed to several monitor screens built into the walls. But the engineers were the members of the crew who had done the hard work of properly calibrating the epsilon drive engines for the flight, and they were literally above and beyond the moon with the success of their efforts.

Freddy and Georgie had taken the deck of cards that was kept around for quick games of poker during down time and were throwing playing cards at each other like confetti. The lack of gravity meant the cards floated and bounced around the room, and the four mice had made a game of trying to flip from one side of the engine room to the other, bouncing into as many floating cards as possible along the way.

Hedda, as the chief engineer, stayed serious and focused on the state of the epsilon drive as it powered down from its first two jumps. Or, at least, as serious as possible given the playing cards bouncing past her pointed ears.

Katasha came down from the bridge, now that the epsilon engine test was done, and joined in the games, somersaulting slowly from one side of the room to the other, while the mice zipped past her, treating the much larger cat like a moving obstacle course.

Yvette grabbed onto two playing cards, one with each paw, and tucked them under her arms on either side. With a little work, she figured out how to flap the cards like wings and flew through the engine room like an awkward, newly fledged bird. It was glorious. All of it was glorious.

In all of her years performing at gymnastics meets and studying architecture, Yvette had never before accomplished anything as amazing as what this team had accomplished today. No one in the solar system had. They had jumped from one planet to the next as easily as Yvette could spring from a tumbling mat to a pair of parallel bars. Like a stone skipping across a lake, they had had skipped across the sky, and now she felt like a resident of the universe, not merely a citizen of a single city, confined within the borders of a country, contained within the omnipresent pull of a planet.

In every way, Yvette was flying.

"Time to land," Captain Kipper's voice came over the internal ship comm system. "The octopus government on Europa has opened a gap in the Jovian moon's shields, and there's a landing pad available for us on the Jupiter-facing side, on top of the new Imperial Star-Ocean Navy base floating on the surface of the world-wide ocean. Follow the coordinates, and let's give our landing gear its first test!"

All the engineers scurried about, getting back into their places, while the playing cards continued to float, rotate, and drift about the engine room.

The landing went smoothly, and the cards drifted slowly downward, towards the floor, as gravity and the very concept of downward returned to the room. Once they'd landed, the cards made a cheerful layer of over-sized confetti, spread across the floor haphazardly, half facing up and half showing the red gingham pattern on their backs.

With the ship successfully landed on a foreign moon, the engineers went about clearing up the cards on the floor. The cards were far less entertaining now that they were all under paw, making the floor slippery. Gravity had turned them into clutter. Katasha and the dachshunds scooped up whole piles of cards with their large paws; the mice carried the cards, held over their heads, one or two at a time to those piles. They had to be careful though, because the gravity was a mere fraction of what they were used to, and escaped cards flipped about the room erratically, flying much farther than they would on Earth.

Once again Captain Kipper's voice filled the room: "Now that we've landed, we'll be bringing aboard our final two crew members—Nioli and Gy'krr are a bonded octopus-raptor pair who have seceded from their own society. I'd like it if everyone aboard exited the ship, so we can all be outside to greet them. Partly, it seems welcoming, but mostly, for most of you this will be your first time setting paw on a world other than Earth, and I don't want any of you to miss that chance before we head on out of our own solar system. The air is breathable, so don't worry about sealing your spacesuits."

Yvette's stomach flipped at the thought of setting paw on an entirely different celestial body, more than it had when gravity had stopped holding her organs down or when space had folded to let *The Lucky Boomerang* hop halfway across the solar system.

Of course, Yvette had known they were landing the ship on Europa. She had seen the dark side of the moon, surrounded by stars, above the galley. She knew what they'd been doing in this engine room... And she could feel the lightness of Europa's gravity, letting her bound across the room in giant leaping steps.

But the engine room was still the same engine room, and knowing something isn't the same as feeling it deep inside, all the way through yourself. Suddenly, her very paws itched with the need to feel a different planet beneath them. Her round ears twitched and tickled at the idea of wind that had never touched a mouse's ears blowing past her.

She stood on the precipice of possibilities that would have seemed like impossibilities only months ago.

Katasha offered the four mice a ride on her shoulders, and all four hopped on—two on each side. With the light gravity, they didn't need Katasha to kneel down or raise them up on her paws. The mice could simply leap from the floor, all the way up to her shoulders.

The Siamese cat seemed pleased with herself as she strolled through the ship's halls with a jaunty, floating step. When the engineers caught up with the main bridge crew at the ship's main entrance—airlock still sealed shut from their flight—Katasha gestured at the mice on her shoulders and threw a self-satisfied grin at Trugger.

The otter gaped and said, "All four of you? On her narrow shoulders at once? When you don't even need a ride due to this ridiculous gravity??? I've been trying to give a ride to all four of you at once for weeks!"

Mulberry, the mouse with markings most similar to Katasha's Siamese patterning, laughed. She was sitting beside Yvette on Katasha's left side, and their tails had tangled together as they'd wrapped around the cat's collar, holding them each securely in position. "I know," she said. "That's why I always chose to run. You wanted it too much."

Trugger comically kicked at the floor and pouted. The kick caused him to float up into the air, and the expression didn't last long. His face was made for merriment, and it brightened into a grin as he held out a webbed paw to Katasha. "Congratulations, you're now officially the mouse passenger wagon."

Katasha's ears skewed, but she accepted the handshake, saying, "What?"

Captain Kipper pressed her paw against the controls for the airlock, and the inner door spiraled open. The tabby cat led the way, and the rest of her crew followed. Once inside the airlock, the captain overrode the safety controls that kept the double doors of the airlock from both opening at the same time when *The Lucky Boomerang* was in the depths of outer space. Cool, humid, salty air rushed in.

Yvette gasped at the feel of the wind on her whiskers and against her furry face. Her ears folded over, protecting themselves from the cacophonous roar of Europa that she only belatedly recognized as the sound of ocean waves rocking and slapping against the sides of the floating otter station.

As Katasha stepped out of the ship, Yvette grasped onto the cat's collar with her tiny paws as well as the curve of her long tail. She hadn't expected to be afraid. She knew that otters and octopi lived on Europa. So, it had to be safe. Or safe enough. Cats had even used to live here—before the New Persia colony was destroyed by the raptor fleet and then the icy surface of the moon had been melted by ancient octopus technology.

Perhaps the fear Yvette felt was an instinctual reaction, something she couldn't possibly have controlled even if she had expected it and tried to push it away. There was a different sky above her, filled with the looming presence of Jupiter; strange, weaving ground below her, bucking slowly like the deck of an ocean liner; and an endless purple-gray ocean stretching in every direction, all around, including down. This world was not a place mice had evolved for. It was not a place mice had ever visited before. And something deep in the pit of Yvette's stomach said that, maybe, it was not a place where mice belonged.

But then an otter—slightly smaller than Trugger but with a grin just as wide—greeted them all with her paws held wide: "Welcome to Europa!"

Trugger rushed forward, shouting, "Jenny!" and hugged the other otter. "Barracuders forever!"

"Barracuders forever," Jenny agreed before stepping back and looking over *The Lucky Boomerang* crew, assembled haphazardly in front of the open airlock, shuffling paws, skewing ears, and mostly staring at the specter of Jupiter hanging impossibly above them.

Jenny stepped up to Captain Kipper, at the front of her crew, took the tabby's hand and said, "Congratulations, Kipper."

"I usually go by 'Captain Kipper' now," Kipper corrected.

Jenny's grin widened and she said, "Then I guess that's *Base Commander Jenny* to you." Both otter and cat laughed, easily, companionably.

Yvette could tell Jenny and Kipper were good friends just from watching them together. She hoped that someday her friendship with Josie would become that easy and straightforward, not knotted up by confusions about their history, priorities, and ambitions. But then, maybe their friendship already looked that way from the outside. She didn't know.

Maybe Kipper and Jenny had as torturous a friendship on the inside of it as the ones Yvette experienced. And yet, watching them talk together, voices lowered now so that the crew couldn't hear it all, she really didn't think so.

Finally Kipper turned back to the crew and said, "Base Commander Jenny has invited us to join the otters and octopi on her base in a meal before we continue our mission."

"And you should really try out swimming in the ocean before you go," Jenny added. "There's a coral reef surrounding the base, and as long as you don't swim past the edge of the coral, the currents will keep you perfectly safe."

"You don't have to tell me twice!" Trugger announced and took off running for the nearest edge of the landing platform.

"Seal your spacesuit!" Kipper called after him. "You don't want it filling with seawater!"

The otter managed to flip his spacesuit's helmet over his head as he ran, and he had it perfectly sealed before diving into the water so smoothly that he barely caused a splash.

Yvette had expected to meet the new crew members, return to the ship, and then be on their way. She didn't know how she felt about hanging out on Europa for swimming and feasting. It seemed almost... hedonistically improper after stealing *The Lucky Boomerang*. It was one thing to steal a spaceship and use it for a mission that might make profoundly important discoveries for the government they'd stolen it from. It was quite something else to steal a spaceship so they could play summer camp on a distant moon.

And yet? Here they were. What harm could a little fun do?

Yvette jumped off Katasha's shoulder with a spin, achieving a longer series of flips and somersaults in the air before landing than she ever could have in Earth's gravity, and bounded after Trugger. By the time she got to the edge of the landing pad, the otter had climbed back out of the ocean and was shedding his spacesuit and uniform, stripping down to the tank top and shorts he wore underneath.

"I want to feel the water," Trugger said by way of explanation. "And these are quick dry fabric anyway." A lot of otters wore quick dry fabrics for all of their clothing.

Trugger dove back into the lapping waves, and Yvette dove after him, keeping her spacesuit on with the helmet sealed. She didn't want to get water in her ears and eyes. She didn't know if it would sting, and she didn't want to find out.

Staring through the faceplate, Yvette saw the riotous colors of the coral reef, growing directly on the side of the floating station and stretching outward into the ocean, some thirty or forty feet below the ocean's surface. She felt the currents pull against her limbs, moving her even as she worked at moving herself. She'd never been much of a swimmer, but one of her more unorthodox gymnastics coaches had believed that practicing underwater routines helped gymnasts ground themselves in their bodies. Not the best coach she'd had. But she'd been young at the time, and swimming had been a nice change of pace from more standard practice methods.

"This floating station is new since the end of the raptor war, right?" Yvette asked, using the radio in her suit to broadcast the question to all the other crew members still wearing their spacesuits. So, probably everyone except Trugger. "How did the coral grow so fast?"

Coral is a notoriously slow-growing species, and yet there was an entire forest of branching, spiky, rough-edged coral in shades of royal purple, sunset orange, and melted butter yellow down there.

"Good question," came back Katasha's voice. The young engineer sounded genuinely interested. "I'll ask one of the Europa otters."

While Yvette waited for the answer, she kept swimming, feeling the pull of the water against her limbs. Trugger swam past her—a sudden blur of brown—and she managed to fall into his wake, picking up speed by following alongside him. Eventually, the other three mice appeared, also swimming and also drawn into the otter's wake. He had become their planet, and they his moons. A tiny representation of Jupiter, Europa, Ganymede, Io, and Callisto.

Yvette told the others of her theory, and Josie chimed up over the radio, "I get to be Io! It's closest to my apricot coloring."

Wendell called Callisto; and Mulberry Europa. Leaving Yvette with Ganymede, a pale gray moon, not too different in coloring from her own soft gray. The four mouse moons held paws in a circle around their otter planet, laughing and spinning and swimming. Yvette thought they were all a little giddy from the combination of joy at their engineering successes, stress at their political transgressions, and sheer dizzying, unbelieving amazement that they were on an entirely different planet.

She could have kept swimming for a long time.

But Katasha's feline voice came over the radio, saying, "The coral is genetically engineered to be fast-growing. One of the technological advancements they found in the ancient octopus computers. Also, Captain Kipper and Base Commander Jenny say that lunch is ready, and you should all come back."

It took a little work for the mouse-moons to capture their otter-planet's attention. Without his spacesuit on, Trugger didn't have a radio speaking into his ear. But eventually, working together, they caught ahold of one of his paws, and when he swirled around to look at them, Yvette signed the situation to him. And then he scooped all four of them up in his webbed paws, swam quickly back to the landing platform, and emerged from the water with them, like some King Kong or Godzilla from an ancient human movie.

Out of the water, the mice took off bounding across the landing platform, while Trugger stayed behind, gathering up the spacesuit he'd discarded for swimming.

Once they'd rounded the side of *The Lucky Boomerang*, Yvette could see a large table, spread with food, and crowded around by otters, chatting with the rest of the ship's crew. Captain Kipper was already seated at the head of the table, beside Base Commander Jenny, deep in rapt conversation.

The other three mice bounded over to the table, reveling in their ability to jump straight from the ground to the tabletop in the low gravity, without needing something to climb or waiting for a lift offered by a bigger animal. But Yvette held back, where she could watch Kipper and Jenny, standing far enough away to be safe from all the wandering paws near the table.

Yvette continued to be fascinated by the friendship between her feline captain and the lutrine base commander. Like most mice, she knew enough about the "Hero of Europa" from news stories—how the tabby cat had grown up in a cattery with her sister and brother, the previous president—that she didn't think the friendship between Kipper and Jenny could have extended back into their childhoods. It couldn't have. Kittens in Uplifted States catteries simply didn't know otters growing up on space stations.

Their friendship wasn't rooted in a long history, and it couldn't be rooted in a similar past. They couldn't have known each other for more than a few years. And yet, there they were, delighted to see each other, connecting at a seemingly deep level, and making choices about the future of the entire solar system together.

Yvette decided she wanted to sit near the head of the table, where she could listen to Kipper and Jenny's conversation. Even if it did mean being the sole mouse up there, as the other three had created an improvised mouse-sized table on top of the otter table out of an overturned serving bowl at the other end.

Yvette bounded past the crowd of otters, now settling into chairs around the table, and landed on the corner of the table by Captain Kipper. A bold, presumptuous move. (Also, a move that was only possible in this low gravity. She simply couldn't be so bold when she depended on a lift from a larger animal to get to the top of a table.) But Yvette wouldn't let herself be turned away. There was no reason to fear her captain—Kipper had been kind and companionable with the whole crew, and the days when mice needed to fear cats simply because of their species were ancient history, back in the Dark Times when humans still walked the Earth.

"Well, hello," Kipper said. Then turning to Jenny she added, "This is Yvette, one of the mice on my engineering team."

"Is it... okay if I join you?" Yvette asked, trying to keep her voice and whiskers from quivering. They apparently hadn't gotten the memo yet from her brain about how she was going to be bold and presumptuous and not let anything get in her way.

Besides, she couldn't quite push aside the knowledge that while jumping right onto the table was a reasonable move for a mouse... it would be extremely uncouth for the larger animals in the crew. And it was weird, albeit necessary, to be held to a different standard.

"Of course, there's plenty of room," Kipper said, casually taking the lid off a butter dish and placing it in front of Yvette as her own improvised table. "Can I grab you anything?" Kipper gestured at the spread of foods in front of them.

Yvette recognized nothing among the dishes. It was all strange colors and textures—something that looked purple and squishy; another dish was filled with something spongy and pale green. She sniffed the air, and while some of it smelled wonderful—fresh and green or salty and fried—it was all still unfamiliar.

"I... don't know what anything is," Yvette admitted.

Jenny smiled as only an otter can—wide and broad and plainly happy. "That's because it's all local—fresh Europa sea life!" She began pointing with a claw at each dish near them, describing what they were. The spongy green one was some kind of sea cucumber, which sounded like a plant but Yvette guessed it was actually an animal. The squishy purple dish was a pile of roasted seaweeds. Altogether, there were too many new, foreign delicacies for Yvette to keep them straight. So, she said, "I'll take a little of anything vegetarian. Is that okay?"

"That's fine." Jenny nodded as she spoke, and then began assembling a collection of tiny servings that she dished out onto the top of the overturned butter dish. When she'd finished, Yvette poked gingerly at the pile of foods with a paw, wishing for the mouse-sized utensils back on *The Lucky Boomerang*. She'd eaten more food with her hands since joining Captain Kipper's crew than she had since being a kit, when her mother had had to force her kicking and squeaking into civilized society one admonishment at a time, and many admonishments per each meal time.

It felt uncouth, grabbing the food with her paws, while the otters, cats, and dogs—even Sequoia and Obsidian!—ate using real utensils.

But she was hungry, and the idea of fresh Europan cuisine was too fascinating to pass up. She grabbed a fistful of glistening, purple, roasted seaweed and held it up to her nose. She took a sniff before testing her teeth on the rubbery strands. They were chewy, salty, and sweet in a very satisfying way, and her whiskers lifted in a grin.

Jenny mirrored Yvette's grin back at her, magnified to ottersize. "It's good, right?"

Yvette nodded, mouth too full of seaweed to squeak. She hoped that if she kept her mouth too busy to speak, Jenny would lose interest in her and would go back to the conversation she'd been having with Kipper. The companionable conversation between two powerful women that had drawn Yvette to this end of the table...

For a while, her plan seemed to be working.

Jenny turned back to Kipper and said, "So, have you kept in touch with Josh?"

Captain Kipper shrugged. "We send each other video messages. He's eloquent and funny, so he makes a good pen pal." Kipper looked down at Yvette and explained, "Josh is a Siamese cat on Mars. I met him when I discovered the hidden purebred cat colony of Siamhalla."

Yvette nodded quickly, trying to acknowledge the information and shake Kipper's focus from her as soon as possible.

"Just a pen pal?" Jenny asked, a teasing tone in her voice.

"Just a pen pal," Kipper agreed. Something in the cat's green eyes made Yvette wonder if there was more between her and Jenny than either of them were letting on. Or maybe even, more than either of them had realized. "Being a space traveler doesn't exactly leave a lot of room for personal relationships anyway. Always flying around."

"Also, being a leader," Jenny added ruefully. "It puts up strange walls between you and the people flying around with you. Or living on an ocean moon with you, as the case may be."

"That's true," Kipper agreed. "I suppose that's been the one silver lining of how the last election went. Alistair, my brother, lost to that hateful Golden Retriever who's trying to shut down my space program. But... It has meant that Alistair finally had time to woo the European squirrel ambassador he'd been will-they-won't-theying with all through his presidency. Now they're properly each other's boyfriends."

"That's nice," Jenny agreed. "I'm happy for them. For better and worse, I can't exactly lose re-election here, since Base Commander wasn't an elected position in the first place..."

Jenny frowned, like she was imagining how her life might be different if she weren't commanding this moon base, and in that moment, Yvette was one hundred percent certain there was an unacknowledged romantic tension between otter and tabby cat. Before Kipper could say anything in response, Trugger popped by unexpectedly, still dripping with Europa ocean water, and interrupted the moment. He said, "Oh, you never know, we held quite a few surprise elections back in our *Jolly Barracuda* days. Remember when Emily got tired of cooking clam chowder over and over again and held a vote to elect herself Selector of What the Chef Cooks As Well as Chef?"

Jenny laughed. "I do. We ate a lot more sushi after that vote."

"Well, first we ate some really bungled clam chowder until Captain Cod stepped down as interim chef." Trugger grabbed a blob of fleshy peach stuff from the table and popped it in his mouth. "Captain Cod was really good at winning those surprise elections."

Kipper's face brightened into a grin again, looking at something further in the distance, and she said, "Well, look, the guest of honor has arrived!" She gestured with a stripey paw toward the far end of the table.

Yvette looked down the long table, seated mostly with otters, to see a large, unusual figure standing at the end. At first, the mouse couldn't make sense of what she was seeing—a confusion of tawny, speckled limbs, all jumbled together, but slowly, her eyes began to pick out the details.

The raptor stood taller than any of the otters or dogs at the table, hunched forward with its feathered, winglike arms close to its sides. Upon its back was settled an octopus—arms wrapped around the raptor's neck like a complicated scarf— whose bare skin had mottled to match the raptor's tawny brown and white feathers. Tentacles and feathers perfectly matched in color and pattern.

Captain Kipper stood up. "Nioli and Gy'krr! Welcome to our crew, and crew, meet our newest members."

CHAPTER 12
KIPPER

Kipper watched the faces of her crew closely as they took in the sight of their newest comrades in arms... and tentacles... and flightless wings. They might be more arms than wings, but those feathery raptor limbs had clearly evolved into bird's wings in some branches of the family tree all of Earth's creatures shared. Well, all of them shared a family tree, except the octopuses. From what Kipper had learned, octopuses were the one sentient race of creatures rattling around this solar system who hadn't actually evolved on Earth. Thank goodness for that, given that octopus technology was behind every piece of her plan to take *The Lucky Boomerang* out into the universe, searching for the wayward humans who'd forgotten to come home and check on the dogs they'd left behind waiting for them. And, you know, the cats too. Though, cats weren't quite as much *waiting*. Certainly not the ones on *The Lucky Boomerang*.

As *The Lucky Boomerang* crew took in the sight of their new members, there wasn't a lot to read on Freddy, Georgie, Hedda, or Katasha's faces, and Kipper wasn't great at reading the expressions of mice or squirrels. Their muzzles were so small and pointy. Amelia though looked incensed. Wary and incensed, eyes glaring past the tiny braids she now sported. She was going to be a difficult one.

Nioli and Gy'krr settled on a bench chair down at the end of the table, looking nervous. Oddly, Kipper could read Nioli's face, or rather the expanse of wrinkled, blotchy, bright orange skin stretched between her wide eyes. Octopus's don't have a lot in terms of actual faces, but they can still be very expressive, especially with their ever-changing coloring. And Kipper had practice reading octopus body language from all the time she'd spent with Emily on *The Jolly Barracuda*.

Nioli looked very nervous.

Kipper supposed that made sense. Part of why the bonded octopus-raptor pair was joining her crew was that they'd been rejected by all corners of their own society. Raptors had been subjugating octopi on Jupiter for an unthinkably long time—far, far longer than cats and dogs had even been uplifted. Longer than humans had been sentient for. Or existed. And now that the Jovian octopi had overthrown their subjugators, most of them had no patience for octopi who had bonded to the raptors who had wielded them like a merely convenient set of extra arms.

But that didn't mean there weren't octopi and raptors who had genuinely created a real, valuable relationship with each other. And those bonded pairs were having a hard time.

This bonded pair in particular—Nioli and Gy'krr—had played an important role in the preparations leading up to the octopus uprising, but had found themselves outcast after the uprising actually took place. Since then, they'd been working on the Europa base with Jenny, unearthing and learning about the ancient octopus technologies hidden here. They'd be an invaluable asset aboard *The Lucky Boomerang*. And Jenny had suggested they'd be more comfortable on Kipper's ship, among a mixed crew composed of all the uplifted species living in the solar system, rather than trying to fit into the edges of their own society which currently didn't want them.

Hopefully, the octopus and raptor societies around and inside of Jupiter would settle themselves out into a more... stable state? Kipper wasn't sure what she was picturing here. Cat and dog society felt like a mess, and it didn't have the centuries of enslavement to reckon with that octopus and raptor society did. Just a couple hundred years of grudges and light discrimination and disenfranchisement. If discrimination and disenfranchisement can ever truly be considered to be light...

Bigotry is bigotry, no matter how small it tries to make itself in order to hide when the reckoning comes.

Kipper took her seat again after seeing that Nioli and Gy'krr had been folded into a conversation at the far end of the table. Nioli's bright orange coloring had subdued some as they'd begun signing with Obsidian who had glued himself to the side of the table with two of his tentacles, entirely forgoing a chair. From what Kipper could read of their signs, they were discussing different dialects of sign language among the octopuses of Jupiter.

Gy'krr seemed to be talking to the cluster of mice seated on top of the table, who were showing a remarkable level of bravery in the face of the raptor's long, razor sharp teeth and massive stature compared to them. Kipper shuddered. She still had nightmares sometimes about the time when she and Trugger had to sneak through an enemy raptor vessel, running for their lives from figures shaped just like Gy'krr, many of them with octopi affixed to their backs just like Nioli.

Kipper knew Gy'krr was a stand-up raptor, vouched for by Jenny and all the other otters on her base, but it was hard to shake the visceral quality of her memories from back then, even though so much time had passed.

"Your other octopus crew member seems to have hit it off with Nioli," Jenny observed.

"Yes, it does seem that way," Kipper agreed. "I'm glad Obsidian won't be the only octopus onboard anymore. I sometimes worry that Trugger and I should have tried harder to find a second squirrel to join the crew... I know it can be hard being the only member of your species on a spaceship. But Sequoia seems to have fit in alright."

The mouse seated near Kipper's plate looked at her quizzically in response to her statement.

"You've probably heard stories about me being the Hero of Europa," Kipper said, trying to address whatever questions Yvette might have without making the mouse actually ask them. "But mostly, I was just lost and confused and surrounded by otters who didn't understand how hard it was for me to be the only cat up here. It's been such a relief having Hedda and Katasha on the crew. That's part of why we made sure to recruit a group of mice who knew each other and would get along. Space is wonderful... but it's also big and cold and will kill you the first chance it gets. You need allies out here. And especially allies who understand where you're coming from."

Yvette looked pensive, and glanced several times down the length of the table toward the other three mice who seemed to be having a lively conversation with Gy'krr. "I hadn't thought of it that way," she squeaked. "Do you think Gy'krr will be alright? Being the only raptor?"

"Gy'krr has been as excited as a trilling songbird looking forward to joining your crew," Jenny said. "I think she's just glad to put some distance between herself and Jupiter honestly."

"And really," Kipper added, "our ship is barely big enough for one raptor onboard. Also, honestly, I'm a lot less worried about individuals from species who've been dominating the space scene for... well, forever. Like Trugger. Sure, he's the only otter aboard *The Lucky Boomerang*, but he's had otters paving his way up here for generations now."

Technically, the octopi had been flying spaceships since

before life on Earth evolved sentience at all, but modern octopus society had been subjugated by raptors or hidden under Earth's oceans for so long that their situation simply wasn't the same.

The rest of the meal passed in a blur of delicious if strange flavors and cheerful jokes, quips, and anecdotes, mostly from the Europa Base otters. Kipper's crew seemed to her to be in fairly good spirits... but tired. That made sense. They'd had a big morning—launching a prototype space vessel, making history for their world, and then being asked to commit treason. Any morning that starts with treason is going to wear on you, at least a little... Even if the panorama of Jupiter's swirly creamsicle clouds does hang impossibly over your head, surrounded by moons and stars that all feel closer than they've ever felt before. The beautiful scene in the sky was a healing balm, but the exhaustion of the morning would still take time to mend.

As the meal began to wrap up, Kipper stood from her chair, signaling to the others that it was time for this phase of their journey to end. She was amazed that standing up was all it took for all of her crew to perk their ears, tilt their heads, or otherwise show that they'd been subtly paying attention to her, waiting for her signal.

"This has been a wonderful meal," Kipper said, speaking in a voice that felt slightly unnatural to her—a little too loud, a little too clear, designed to be heard by everyone at the table. "But we have a mission to attend to."

"Before you go—" Jenny rose from her seat as well and waved her paws in an encouraging way at one of the otters further down the table. He got up and scurried away, as if he was going to fetch something. "—Captain Cod left a little something for you when *The Jolly Barracuda* was last here."

"A little something?" Kipper echoed, bewildered and a little troubled. Captain Cod was an unpredictable one.

The otter, who Kipper now recognized as Felix, staggered his way back to the table holding a large, rectangular, flat package, wrapped in a colorful patterned paper. The pattern was tiny rocket ships, cleverly tessellated together so half of them were flying one way, and the other half the other.

Felix brought the package over to Kipper and leaned it against the table.

"It's... kind of large. You know spaceships are tight," Kipper said, poking at the paper with a claw.

"Open it!" Trugger cried. "We have to see what's in it!"

So Kipper slashed the paper with her claws, revealing the object underneath.

A painting.

Kipper's heart leapt into her throat. She recognized the painting. It was one of the first things she'd seen onboard *The Jolly Barracuda*, during her first ever day in space. She placed her paw gently on its surface, protected by the same plexiglass shielding that it had had back on *The Jolly Barracuda*. It felt like she was touching the surface of nostalgia itself.

The painting was of an old-style Earth sailing ship, complete with billowing sails, crewed by a wild mix of animals, many of whom had never reached sentience—a giraffe, an alligator, and a flamingo—in addition to the more standard otter, dog, cat, squirrel, mouse and even a human, wearing a wide captain's hat. The ship sailed on a starry expanse of sky, swirling with purple and blue. It was fantastical, whimsical, and everything she remembered loving about *The Jolly Barracuda*. It captured the heart of what she was trying to do with *The Lucky Boomerang*— bring all the species she could together into one cohesive crew, exploring the sky.

But then a horrible thought occurred to Kipper, "Is this painting... it's not still..." She didn't want to say 'stolen," because Captain Cod and his crew were touchy about that. Technically, they'd never stolen the paintings. They just hadn't finished delivering them to actual buyers. For years. The artists who'd painted them were furious.

"No, no," Felix said, "I asked the captain about that, and he paid for this one. It's not in transit anymore. It's made its way to its final owner."

Kipper smiled. "You'll have to help me figure out where we can hang it on *The Lucky Boomerang* before we take off."

CHAPTER 13
SEQUOIA

Sequoia felt like she'd spent the whole meal on Europa playing some sort of game with Amelia, catching each others' eyes and then glancing away, trying not to get caught looking at each other. Except, she wasn't sure if it was something they were both doing, or if it was all in her own head. She didn't know why the mop dog had stayed with the crew when she was so clearly opposed to everything Captain Kipper was doing. And it made her feel all fluttery inside.

Or maybe that was the low gravity.

Every time Sequoia flipped her tail, she felt like she was going to float away in this low Europa gravity. Her tail felt like a sail, like on that fantastical painting Captain Kipper had been given by her old captain.

In spite of the joy of seeing Jupiter hanging over her head, and the deliciously weird local kelp dishes, Sequoia was relieved when she set paw back on *The Lucky Boomerang*. It had started to feel like home to her. And as she settled back into her post on the bridge, she felt a new kind of fluttering in her heart—one that had nothing to do with inconvenient crushes or unusual gravity.

It was all about stars.

Little yellow stars that could provide warm sunlight to a scattering of planets around them; white dwarf stars that twinkled prettily but were too cold to provide a home to any habitable planets; and red giant stars overflowing with too much heat, scorching the planets that used to rely on them. Sequoia loved them all. Especially the pulsars with their uneven light and binary stars that circled each other forever in a dance of gravity, drawn forever together but also held apart.

Like Sequoia and Amelia at lunch...

No.

Sequoia was not going to think about a foolish dog when there were stars waiting to fill her senses.

The rest of the bridge crew took their places more belatedly than Sequoia. They'd stayed to see the painting installed in *The Lucky Boomerang's* central corridor—the only space with enough blank wall space for it to fit. Most of the ship was too compact, contorted around all the technology it took to keep it afloat in the sky for a big ol' painting to fit.

The ascent from Europa was quick, and then *The Lucky Boomerang* shot through the emptiness of space, away from Jupiter, away from Earth, away even from the sun. Away from everything that squirrels and all the other animals aboard had ever known.

And then came Sequoia's moment to shine.

"Sequoia," Captain Kipper said, "please set a course for our first epsilon-drive jump out of the solar system."

Sequoia's heart raced. She was going to go visit the stars. *Her stars.* The stars she'd loved since she was a kit. "Do you have anywhere in particular in mind, Captain?" Sequoia asked, barely able to believe she was asking those words. Barely able to believe any of this was happening.

"You know the mission," Captain Kipper replied, looking comfortable in her captain's seat. "And you know the stars. That's why you're here. We have fuel for several dozen jumps before we'll have to go home, so why don't you start us out easy. Somewhere not too close to any given star, just for safety as we get started. But also, you know, maybe a cluster where there are a couple of stars that might support life around them? Maybe where... humans might have headed?" The captain's voice faltered over the word "humans."

Talking about humans felt a little bit like talking about unicorns, or dragons, or vampires, or ghosts. Something less than real. Or maybe, more than real. Because sometimes, myths are more powerful than reality.

"Got it," Sequoia said. She'd been given free reign to take the ship anywhere outside the solar system. And she knew the perfect place. A cluster of nice, mid-sized yellow stars that she personally thought of as the Acorn Cluster. The way they were all bunched up together made her think of acorns clustered together on a branch. Any of those stars could have planets orbiting them. Possibly nice, habitable planets.

Sequoia chose a location just outside of the cluster, allowing the safe distance Captain Kipper had requested, and programmed it into the ship's computer. She truly couldn't believe that her love of stars and cataloguing them had led to her being the navigator on an interstellar spacecraft. It made no sense. It was beyond her wildest imaginings. And yet it had happened. She was here, and she was about to be *there*. Right outside the Acorn Cluster.

"Course plotted, Captain," Sequoia said, feeling more like a kit roleplaying one of the characters on *Tri-Galactic Trek* than a full-grown adult squirrel doing a real job.

"Onward and outward," Captain Kipper replied, and everyone on the bridge giggled, recognizing the catchphrase of the Sphynx cat captain on *Tri-Galactic Trek*. So, Sequoia wasn't the only one feeling like a kit pretending to be on a TV space show.

Sequoia supposed they all felt a little flustered and out of their element at this moment. They were about to do something they'd only seen happen in stories before.

Sequoia pressed the button locking her coordinates in place, and the epsilon jump sequence began.

Just like the first two jumps, a sensation of largeness filled Sequoia, starting deep in her belly and growing outward, as if she were expanding into a star herself. A squirrel star, red and bright. Then the sensation flipped, snapping her back to herself. It happened too fast. Sequoia would have lived in the moment between the beginning and end of an epsilon jump if she could have. She'd have chosen to be a star herself, like all the glittering, winking, bright spots in the sky which she loved so much.

But once again, all too fast, she was a squirrel.

A squirrel light-years away from every other squirrel. Light-years away from where she'd begun. The thought was dizzying.

Then her eyes raised from the control-panel in front of her to the vid-screen dominating the room. Those tiny specks of light, mere diamond chips strewn on an infinite black sand beach, had grown. Perhaps, if you didn't know the stars as well as Sequoia did, they'd still look like nothing much. Spots of light. They were still far away. But so much closer. And Sequoia could make out the warmth, the yellowness of their light, with her bare eyes, without need for complicated tools that magnified them or read their spectrographic footprint. She could see them. For herself.

She'd been born for this moment. She'd dreamed of it so many times that the moment itself seemed to create beats across her life, echoing back to all her kit-hood dreams, making them retroactively prophetic.

"So... why here?" Amelia asked, voice echoing across the otherwise reverently silent bridge. "What made you pick these stars?"

Sequoia's eyes flitted reluctantly away from the viewscreen

to glare daggers at the scruffy mop dog who'd interrupted her moment of transcendence.

"I mean, there's no record of where humans went," Amelia continued. "I'm no expert, but I've read enough pop science books about archaeology and ancient human studies to know that anything like records of where they went were completely lost during the Dark Times. No one's been able to decode the remnants of computers left from those times. So, what, did you just point at the sky and go, 'There! Let's fly there!' Or is there some method to this madness?"

The dog's voice had a mocking tone that made Sequoia's thin red fur bristle all over her neck and shoulders. If she were a porcupine, she'd have been shooting quills at Amelia out of fury. Even though porcupines don't actually do that. She'd have found a way.

"We're not expecting to find humans on our first jump, Amelia," Captain Kipper said with just enough condescension in her voice to ameliorate Sequoia's fury some. At least the annoying dog was being spoken down to. Like she deserved.

"We're expecting to find information," Sequoia snapped primly. "And there's an abundance of it here. Radio waves that will take years to reach our own solar system, assuming they ever do. If they're being broadcast directionally, they might only be findable out this far. The background noise here is a veritable soup of information."

"Info soup!" Trugger exclaimed. "Less delicious than clam chowder, but potentially much more valuable."

"Much more," Captain Kipper agreed. "We can stay here a few hours, absorbing and analyzing the data available. But then I'll expect you to pick our next location. Our fuel gives us several dozen jumps, and our life support supplies give us several months. But our patience won't last forever. I mean, yes, I imagine some of us would be happy analyzing the star data we can find out here forever—"

Based on the way the captain was looking at her, Sequoia suspected the captain knew that her squirrel navigator fell into exactly that category.

"—but there's a lot of space out here, and our chances of finding something interesting will be higher if we can cover more ground in the time available."

Sequoia wasn't sure that was true. She could spend the next month analyzing the background noise in this one spot, and she might have as much chance of happening on a stray radio signal with useful information as she'd have if they hopped to a new location every few hours. Space is big, and when you're surrounded by it in every direction, there's a lot of information to analyze. That's why astronomers could stay busy on Earth for entire lifetimes, even though the planet wasn't hopping its way through the universe like a frantic frog.

There are always more corners of the sky to stare at, analyze, and dig into ever more deeply.

Even so, this corner was already one of Sequoia's favorites. She truly believed that one or more of these yellow stars would prove to have planets, and she hoped at least one of those planets would have life on it.

So, she needed to hunker down and get to work if she was going to prove the Acorn Cluster deserved more of their time than a few hours.

CHAPTER 14
YVETTE

After a week of hopping across the galaxy, cataloguing stars and background radiation signatures everywhere they went, *The Lucky Boomerang* wasn't feeling like such a lucky vessel to the hopeful crew aboard. They'd found no sign of humans. No sign of alien life. Nothing.

Just stars.

They were beautiful stars, and the squirrel navigator still seemed to be happy once she'd accepted the captain's insistence that the crew was better off collecting data across a multitude of different sites rather than digging really deeply into one site.

Yvette could see Sequoia's point—even knowing very little about astronomy, she was willing to believe that trying to deeply understand one new point of view could potentially have more value than shallowly understanding a couple dozen. But she also knew that dozens of shoddy snapshots were going to look more impressive to all the animals back on Earth than a single, highly detailed painting. Unless, of course, that painting had an actual human in it, like the one Captain Cod had gifted Captain Kipper of the sailing ship.

Yvette had spent a lot of time staring at that oil painting during the last week. And thinking about the things Captain

Kipper had said about being the only one of your species in space. Or in any place.

Yvette hadn't set out to be an astronaut. It wasn't the fulfilment of a lifelong dream like it had been for Sequoia, Katasha, Hedda, or Georgie. And originally, she'd planned to make the money she earned working for *The Lucky Boomerang* and return home a relatively rich mouse. Devote herself full-time to architecture, without feeling beholden to take the best paying jobs rather than the most fulfilling ones.

But now...

She was starting to see herself as something of a pioneer or potential role-model. And she wasn't sure she was comfortable with that. But she also wasn't sure she felt right about simply declining a mantle that had been laid on her shoulders. If she continued working in space, even just staying on with *The Lucky Boomerang*, would she be making it easier for more mice to find their way into space travel? Perhaps mice who *had* always dreamed of it, but hadn't seen a path to making it possible before she paved the way?

She thought she might. And the possibility... it was enough to make it worthwhile. Maybe she didn't care as much about the stars or finding humans as some of the other crew members, but she did enjoy the complexity of the spaceship's design, and she enjoyed thinking about ways to improve it. Spaceship design wasn't exactly like architecture, but it was related. And she thought her background in architecture might actually be helpful for designing future spaceships with the crew's comfort in mind. She could make a career out of that and be happy.

And all of that would be easier if she could convince Josie, Mulberry, and Wendell to stay on with *The Lucky Boomerang* as well.

So, while the other three mice and two cats of the engine room had fallen back on the poker games they'd played before liftoff to amuse themselves, Yvette had been staring at the painting in the hallway, searching for inspiration.

Sequoia and the dachshunds (who had turned out to also have studied astronomy) were busy analyzing the star data *The Lucky Boomerang* had been collecting, and Obsidian had fallen deeply into an ongoing conversation with Nioli and Gy'krr about their respective societies and lives within them up until now. From what Yvette had glimpsed of their conversation, it looked like the kind of heart-to-heart that college freshmen have after three in the morning during their first weeks of life away from the homes where they'd grown up. Their first time truly stepping into a new way of life.

Being on *The Lucky Boomerang* was a little like doing college over again—a whole new place with new people, and once you get there, it becomes your whole world.

But you graduate from college. What would graduating from *The Lucky Boomerang* even look like?

Yvette kind of hoped it would look like the painting of the sailing ship. *Adventure. Camaraderie. And great beauty.*

But she feared it would look more like *The Lucky Boomerang* itself—*plain gray metal arranged into boxy shapes with sharp corners and nothing fitting quite right.*

But maybe, she could make it fit better.

Yvette decided what her first step would be.

As much as the mice had come to love flying through the zero gee, using wings they'd sewn together out of scraps cut from an extra blanket during the ship's first day of star-hopping, there was no doubt that it made designing living and work spaces more difficult than if the ship had gravity. Of course, providing a natural replacement for gravity—by spinning the ship to create centripetal forces pushing everyone and every-thing inside toward the outer edges of the ship—would involve a complete redesign.

But there was another option—Nioli and Gy'kyrr had

brought plans with them, recently uncovered at the Europa Base, for an artificial gravity generator.

Yvette thought it was time to get to work on building one...

Yvette flapped her fabric wings and flew right into the middle of the floating poker game in the middle of the engine room. All of the players stared at her past their hands of cards, and hovering among the drifting poker chips, she folded her wings and said, "Come on, we can play poker on Earth. We're in deep space right now! Let's take advantage of that!"

"How?" Josie asked drily. "You want to play some sort of zero gee sport to pass the time instead?"

"I don't want to just pass the time," Yvette replied. "I want to further the cause of interstellar space travel."

Josie's eyes narrowed, crinkling the creamy orange fur of her brow. "And how do you propose we do that?"

"I want to build the artificial gravity generator that Nioli and Gy'krr brought plans for."

"But I like the zero gee," Mulberry said, wrinkling her dark-furred nose. "We can get anywhere without help in this gargan-tuan ship."

"Sure," Yvette agreed, shoving a big red disk of a poker chip that had floated up to her out of the way. "The zero gee is convenient for us while we're on a vessel built to accommodate larger animals, but what if mice ever made their own vessels? And it's not like you have to turn the artificial gravity all the way up to Earth levels, just because you *can*. We could keep it at a nice Europa-like level."

"I suppose that's true," Mulberry admitted, looking intrigued.

"Like I said, this is about furthering the cause of space trav-el," Yvette insisted. "Progress! Technological advancement!" The others looked skeptical. "Impressing everyone you meet for the rest of your life because you can say you were among the first group to build a working artificial gravity generator this side of the asteroid that wiped out dinosaurs on Earth?"

"Yeah, okay." Josie folded her hand of playing cards, dividing it into two stacks as she did, and then used those stacks as supplemental wings to fly to the pile of chips floating in the middle. "Help us clear this card game away, and then we can dig through the backup supplies and materials in the cargo bay to see if we really have all the supplies we'd need. Are Nioli and Gy'krr onboard with your plan? 'Cause, they're kind of the experts, and we'd probably need their help."

"I'll get them onboard," Yvette said, feeling a lightness in her heart that had nothing to do with the lack of gravity in the room and everything to do with one of her oldest friends agreeing to work on a project with her.

Next Yvette turned to the two cats who'd been playing cards with the three mice, but she didn't have to say anything, just throw a quizzical look their way.

"Oh, you had me at 'further the cause of interstellar space travel,'" Katasha said.

And Hedda said, "I'm always up for building something." The calico's golden eyes twinkled. She was an engineer through and through. "The only reason I hadn't started already is that these space jumps every few hours have me expecting something exciting to happen any moment..."

"And then it doesn't," Katasha finished the thought for Hedda, adding a dose of wryness to it. "Because it's a doggarned big galaxy out here, and if humans had really been planning to come back, they'd have done so by now." She rolled her clear blue eyes. She was a cat with strong opinions on dog religions. "I'm all for exploring space, but looking for humans is a silly publicity stunt if you ask me."

"You don't think we'll find anything out here?" Josie asked. She was still trying to help gather the poker cards and chips together, but her efforts were much less effective than those of the cats, whose paws were as large as a whole mouse.

"I don't know," Katasha admitted. "But I think we're far more likely to find aliens than humans."

"Really weird, impossible to understand aliens!" Hedda added gleefully with the kind of Cheshire grin that could make a mouse shudder all the way to the tip of her tail if she thought it were aimed hungrily at her.

"Yeah, like space blimps who feed on nebula gasses or sentient rocks that vibrate in harmony with each other to communicate!" Katasha agreed.

There was something mesmerizing for a mouse about watching two cats play together, even if it was only verbally. Terrifying, beautiful giants who somehow managed to be benevolent in spite of the genetic, pre-uplift history of their species.

Civilization is a wonderful thing. Yvette was definitely a fan. She much preferred exploring space with these cats to hiding from them in some dingy hole in a wall while they hunted her on four paws.

"Okay, then," Yvette said, spreading her fabric wings. "I'll see the rest of you in the cargo bay, after I check in with Nioli and Gy'krr."

The other mice and cats waved her on, and Yvette flew away toward the barracks. When she got there, she found Gy'krr curled into a tight ball of feathers, nesting on his cramped bunk. Nioli wasn't in sight. Yvette guessed the octopus—and probably the other octopus, Obsidian—was in the tank of water that served as their bunk, closer to the center of the ship. Every time Yvette had seen them, all week long, they'd been signing at each other, rapidly twisting and contorting their tentacles into ever-evolving series of signs. Yvette had done a pretty good job of learning the octopus half of Swimmer's Sign so she could understand Obsidian when he talked, but either they weren't sticking with just Swimmer's

Sign, or their tentacles simply moved too fast and fluidly for her to keep up.

With a deep breath to steel herself, Yvette decided she should try figuring out if the raptor curled up in her bunk was actually asleep... or just resting. Yvette severely doubted she'd be brave (or foolish) enough to risk waking a sleeping raptor up. She'd known plenty of mice in her time who woke up grumpy and snappish if their sleep was disturbed. Her own mother included. She didn't want to see what a grumpy and snappish bird of prey was like. At her size, Yvette would be less than a mouthful to Gy'krr. A raptor like that made cats seems positively unthreatening.

With a few flaps of her fabric wings, Yvette fluttered like a little fairy through the room until she was hovering only inches away from the raptor's speckled feathers. "Ah... uh... ahem?" she managed to squeak out.

The ball of feathers shifted, uncurling, until Yvette could see a giant golden eye staring at her from its middle. Gy'krr had managed to curl herself completely around, until her head was tucked under her arm, much as it would have been if she were a bird and her arm were an actual wing. "Yes?" the raptor hissed.

"The rest of us... from the engine room... the mice and cats, that is, we, uh, thought we'd try building the artificial gravity generator that you brought plans for? And, uh, we'd like your help?" Yvette wasn't thrilled with how her already squeaky-sounding voice rose into a shrill, pleading whine at the end of her sentence. But there was something very deep inside her brain screaming at her to be afraid of this raptor. Birds of prey are nightmare fuel for mice.

The bird of prey uncurled further, lifting her head up and blinking those giant golden eyes. "Really?" Gy'krr's voice sounded oddly hopeful, almost pleading.

"Well, yeah," Yvette said, flapping her wings a few times. She couldn't help wanting to back away from the raptor's mouth, with its sharp teeth, even if she was here to talk to the owner of that mouth. "We engineers are all kind of bored at this point, waiting to find out if... well, we find anything out here. So, we thought, why not? And you should know more about those plans than any of the rest of us..."

Gy'krr blinked her golden eye again, and when it reopened, Yvette saw the clear gleam of a smile there. "Yes, yes, please, I would like something to do while my octopus self is busy."

"Awesome!" Yvette said. She wondered about Gy'krr's use of the phrase "octopus self," but she didn't want to press her luck right now. Maybe she could ask about it later. She knew Gy'krr and Nioli were a bonded pair, but she really didn't know what that meant. "Do you, uh, want to come to the cargo bay and help us figure out if we have the right supplies?"

"Yes," Gy'krr agreed, looking much more lively. "I will follow?"

"Sure," Yvette said, feeling unsure about the idea of having a giant bird of prey following her through the halls of the spaceship. That said, it was probably easier than trying to dodge about next to her in this zero gravity space.

The mouse began flapping her fabric wings and got up enough momentum to soar through the barracks, down the hall, and right into the cargo bay. Nothing was very far away from anywhere else aboard a spaceship. With all the empty space outside, it seemed kind of ironic to Yvette how much space inside was at a premium. But then, livable, breathable space is worth a whole lot more than vacuum.

Inside the cargo bay, Mulberry and Wendell were poring over a computer pad with the blueprints for the gravity generator while the cats and Josie dug through the carefully stored backup supplies. They had already started a floating pile of loose pieces, no longer carefully stored away, ready for them to build with.

"We aren't going to actually need any of these pieces for the main engine are we?" Josie asked, carrying a spool of thread-thin silver wire from a drawer at the side of the room and toward the floating pile in the middle. "I mean, this stuff is all for if something in the ship breaks, right? So, we probably shouldn't use it up... in case we need it."

Katasha turned to gaze at the pile with her clear blue, calculating Siamese eyes. Her dark ears skewed. "I mean, worst case scenario, we tear apart the gravity generator and scavenge the pieces we need back, right?"

Hedda shrugged her splotchy calico shoulders which were bare under the rolled up arms of her blue uniform. "The engine works. I don't think we're going to actually need any of this."

"Unless we get hit by a space rock in just the wrong way," Wendell muttered in his tiny voice.

"Well, if we do need it back, it'll still be here," Hedda argued. "Like Katasha said."

Yvette was troubled to realize that Wendell had a point—yanking pieces back out of an artificial gravity generator would be a lot less efficient than just using fresh new pieces that were properly stored in the cupboards and drawers meant for them. And a few minutes of inefficiency could mean life or death out here in space.

That said, she really didn't want to side with Wendell against the feline engineers. And more than that, she didn't want to go back to sitting on her paws while that squirrel navigator hopped all over the galaxy searching for needles in a haystack.

Besides, Yvettte suspected that the feline engineers' cavalier attitude came from knowing, deep down, that if something went wrong, a few minutes wouldn't make a difference, because the kind of things that go wrong with an interstellar engine don't take a few minutes. They happen in a matter of seconds. And it's better not to think about them.

"I'm sure it'll be fine," Yvette said. "And look!" She gestured at Gy'krr as the bird of prey glided into the room, far too large to need a mouse to draw attention to her. "Gy'krr's here to help us!"

Gy'krr's long neck seemed to shrink, drawing her angular head back into her feathered shoulders. "Well... help... yes. But..."

"What's wrong?" Yvette asked, risking flying back closer to the raptor with a few flaps of her fabric wings.

"Not so helpful with just..." Gy'krr held out her talons, as if there were something wrong with them, like they were less a part of her and more just useless lumps attached to her. "Am used to having tentacles. Not so... dexterous now."

Josie's round, orange ears flattened against her back. On a mouse flattened ears was more of a stricken look and less like the annoyed expression cats got when their ears flattened. "Are you saying you don't know how to be helpful without Nioli to be your... uh... hands?"

"No," Gy'krr objected, yellow eyes narrowing. But then her feathers ruffled and she admitted, "Yes. Am used to being... only half. Other half self busy now."

"Don't worry about it," Yvette said, trying to avoid anything going wrong with her plans here. "You have mice to be your hands now."

"And cats!" Katasha exclaimed, happily digging through the pile of wires, gears, gaskets, and whatnot floating in the middle of the room. She looked like a kitten pawing at a pile of string. Perfectly happy, completely entranced. "Now what do we start with?"

Wendell began reading from the blueprints with Mulberry occasionally correcting him. Yvette helped the cats and Josie begin assembling the disparate pieces, and eventually, Gy'krr found herself drawn into the process. The raptor stayed back from the others, keeping her talons tucked beside her as if they really were folded wings and not just feathered arms ending in claw-like hands. But she helped by pointing out ways the others could assemble the pieces more efficiently, based on what she'd learned about other ancient octopus technologies at the Europa base. Her presence was definitely an asset, and as the building went along, the raptor even began to warm up and talk about her life a bit with the others.

Yvette didn't know if the others were as fascinated by Gy'krr as she was, but she did notice that everyone quieted down whenever the raptor started to speak. She was the only one of them who'd ever been inside the clouds of Jupiter, onboard a raptor vessel, or had her consciousness technologically joined with an octopus.

Yvette found the symbiotic relationship Gy'krr described with Nioli utterly fascinating. It sounded somewhere between a marriage of best friends; a lifelong collaboration between a musician and a lyricist; and something just utterly indescribable if you hadn't experienced it yourself. Though, it did make Yvette think of her brief experiences doing partner gymnastics— needing to coordinate her every move with another person, totally reliant on the other mouse fulfilling her parts of the routine.

Yvette couldn't tell if she was deeply jealous of the bond Gy'krr described having with Nioli... or kind of viscerally horrified by it. It would be confusing and intrusive enough to have one's mind melded with another of one's own species. At least then you'd understand how all the different limbs and senses worked. Add on a bunch of tentacles and sucker discs that could literally taste the things they touched and change color with their mood? And goodness, that sounded more like a drug trip to Yvette than a partnership.

Speaking of drug trips, the ship-wide intercom clicked on, and Captain Kipper's voice spoke over it: "Crew, please prepare for another epsilon jump in five minutes."

"I don't know how valuable the star data they're collecting is," Wendell grumbled, "but these jumps are very disruptive."

Yvette's hopes of keeping Wendell with the crew had been diminishing more and more. He clearly really hated the sensation of epsilon jumping, and while he seemed to be enjoying his role reading out instructions from the blueprints, he didn't seem especially excited about the project itself.

Fortunately, Josie and Mulberry had been having a great time brainstorming with the cats about how an artificial gravity generator could be used to create an uneven gravity field aboard a spaceship, making some portions zero gee and others low gee depending on what was most convenient for the activities meant to take place there.

Yvette was pretty sure that Mulberry had fallen so deeply in love with life as a moustronaut that she'd stay with *The Lucky Boomerang* whether any of the other mice did or not. And if Mulberry and Yvette both stayed? Josie would probably stay too.

If Yvette could have seen herself now—hanging out with her old best friend, building an artificial gravity generator on a spaceship hundreds of lightyears from Earth—back when she'd been lonely, bitter, and isolated over the last few years... She never would have believed it. She'd been starting to give up on friendship and happiness. They'd seemed too hard to her. As impossible for her as jumping from one star-system to another.

Neither of which had turned out to be impossible at all. Life has a way of being surprising.

CHAPTER 15
SEQUOIA

"You need to sleep," Captain Kipper insisted to the bleary-eyed, scraggle-tailed squirrel, mere minutes after the latest epsilon jump. "I can make that an order if you'd like. And it doesn't have to be more than a nap, but if you don't lie down in the barracks and close those eyes for a while, you're not allowed on the bridge anymore."

Sequoia glared at the screen of data in front of her, flooding with new numbers in this new location that represented stars she hadn't had time to get to know well yet. She didn't dare look up at the captain. She knew she'd keep glaring, and she figured that glaring at her captain was a bad idea. She'd probably end up ordered to sleep for a solid eight hours instead of just catching a nap.

Napping was all she'd done, all week long. And mostly only when Captain Kipper made her. She needed to study these stars; she needed to study them before the ship jumped away from them again. She needed to be here, on the bridge, studying her stars. Because she didn't know when she'd ever get to do something like this again. And the thought of being stuck in the solar system, unable to hop about the galaxy like a water-skipper on the top of a lake was unthinkable to her now. She hated that she'd ever been trapped on a single world, and she never wanted to do that to herself again.

"I'll walk her to the barracks," Amelia woofed.

Sequoia laughed, an unhinged sound. "*Walk!* Hah, right. You mean, *float.*" But she didn't struggle when the scruffy dog's paws laid on her shoulders, pulling her gently away from her post.

The two of them floated down the halls of the ship together, Amelia continuing to guide Sequoia with her paws. The dog's paws felt solid and soothing against Sequoia's back. She knew the stars she'd been studying were real, physical objects out there in space, but to her, all week, they'd been numbers and graphs on computer screens. Ephemeral. Phantom images of real objects. And she loved them with all her heart, but studying them was possibly making her lose her mind a little bit. She felt like a kitten who'd been chasing the red light of a laser pointer all week, with no actual toys she could get her paws on and sink her claws into.

She was starting to realize—and this should have been obvious, but somehow it hadn't been—that the stars didn't love her back.

By the time the dog and squirrel made it into the barracks, the sensation of floating made Sequoia feel like she was already dreaming, even though she still wasn't asleep. She was too wound up, deep inside, to sleep. No matter what the captain ordered.

Regardless, Sequoia let Amelia help her into a bunk and strap the restraints around her body that would stop her from floating right back out of the bunk.

Then the squirrel watched as the scruffy dog secured herself into the bunk across the way.

The dog and squirrel stared at each other. Unblinking.

Sequoia started to giggle, because it felt like a staring contest and she couldn't think of anything sillier than launching a bunch of astronauts into the sky so that they could skip to the other side of the galaxy and have staring contests.

"You're not sleeping," Amelia observed drily.

"Nope!" Sequoia agreed cheerfully.

"You're not even trying."

"Hey now," Sequoia said. "You don't know that. You just don't know how hard sleep is for me."

"Apparently." The mop dog picked at the straps holding her in her bunk. "You do realize that all the data the ship's gathering will still be available when we get home and that the ship keeps gathering data while you sleep, and on top of all of that, those dachshund brothers are sifting through all those numbers right now anyway."

"Yeah..." Sequoia agreed grimly.

"So what's the big deal? Why won't you—or can't you—sleep?" Amelia stopped fidgeting with her restraining straps and turned her warm brown eyes toward Sequoia.

The squirrel almost gasped at the power of those brown eyes. She hadn't realized how little the dog looked directly at her until their eyes locked, and it almost felt like too much. It wasn't that Amelia didn't look at her... not quite. But never so directly. Flitting looks. Angled looks. This gaze was direct, and it was filled with heat. Just like a star.

Amelia really wanted to understand what was driving Sequoia to mad, sleep-deprived depths.

"Studying the stars is all I've ever done that I cared about," Sequoia said, her tone even and plain. She was speaking her simple truth. The core of who she was. "It's all I've ever wanted to do. And now, I have the freedom to study the stars from new angles, from a degree of closeness... I can..." She faltered. It was all too big to explain. Like the stars. Astronomers and astrophysicists tried to capture them in long lists of numbers and equations. But beyond all of that... They were so big, it was almost incomprehensible to small mammals like squirrels and dogs.

Sequoia was losing Amelia's interest, and she could see the dog's brown eyes straying.

Sequoia drew a deep breath and started over, from a new angle. "When I was a kit, there was a total solar eclipse. My family had to take the train for three days to get to a place that would experience totality, and it was the most fun I'd ever had. My cousins and I stormed up and down the train, exploring the dining car and the lounge car and..." She shook her head, this part was beside the point. "When we got there, we stayed with a distant relative—a squirrel who had married an otter—and we all set up folding chairs in their wide backyard, right beside a babbling stream, and we kits kept playing, but..."

Amelia was staring steadily at her again.

"We made a special viewer out a cardboard box and wore special glasses, so we could watch the moon eating away at the sun, taking bigger and bigger bites out of it." Sequoia's voice had grown hollow and wavery, like she was channeling the memory of her past self. "The other kits thought it was fun, but I was entranced by the changing shape of the little yellow disk in the viewer. And then totality came. The air turned chill. Everything turned strangely twilight in the middle of the day. We took our glasses off, because the sun was blocked completely behind the moon, and we didn't need them anymore. And—" Her voice choked off, remembering the moment that had come to define her life.

"I remember seeing an eclipse when I was a pup," Amelia said, trying to encourage the squirrel to continue. "But I wasn't anywhere near totality, so I only sort of saw it. I saw videos of the actual totality."

"It's not the same," Sequoia said. She said it quickly, but

somehow, she didn't snap the words. Just rushed them. "When you're there... It's like the distance between the Earth and the sun suddenly becomes real and understandable. A tangible distance that your brain can understand. There's you, small and furry and full of blood rushing through your body, pushed and pulled by a beating heart. But then above you... There's the moon, and it's not just a disc in the sky. It's a real, solid object, a giant round rock, hanging impossibly in space between you and the sun. And suddenly, the sun feels like a real thing. Huge, and fiery, and golden, just peeking out from around the edges of the moon. Almost like something you could touch, if you could just reach high enough... *It feels real.*" Nothing else had ever felt that real. She couldn't stress those words strongly enough to communicate what she had felt. Instead, feeling her failure to capture the moment she remembered so vividly, she muttered, "And it never did before. It never felt real, and even when you were looking right up at the sky, you simply didn't know how much you were missing." Sequoia's voice choked again.

Silence filled the space between the dog and squirrel the way that emptiness filled the space between the Earth, moon, and sun.

Sequoia wrung the final words of her story out of herself: "Then eight minutes later it's over, and you can't believe you'll never get to feel that close to the sun ever again."

"There have been other eclipses since then," Amelia objected.

Sequoia shook her head. "I couldn't become some kind of junky eclipse chaser, throwing all of my money into traveling around the world following the eclipses for a few minutes here and there of that high."

"So, instead you devoted your whole life to studying stars?" Amelia sounded skeptical of that trade, and for the first time, Sequoia wondered if her whole career had been nothing more than a pale imitation of what she'd really wanted to do: chase eclipses.

And yet, her career had brought her here. Up among the stars.

And just like those eight minutes of totality, this trip would end soon. And she couldn't stand losing that feeling of being close to the stars once again. She'd been chasing that feeling her whole life.

"I... I don't know what it is, really," Sequoia mumbled, mostly to herself. "Was it the chill in the air? The twilight? And now, is it the zero gravity? Could I just go on vacation to Moonville Funpark and bounce in the low-gee chamber every couple of years? I mean, this drive, this compulsion I feel... it just doesn't make sense..."

"That it's really the stars pulling you toward them?" Amelia asked.

"Yeah, I mean, they're all still just specks in the sky around us. Even when we're up here with them." Sequoia was as befuddled by her own obsession and the paradoxes within it as anyone else could be. She'd experienced it, growing with her as she'd grown up, but she still didn't understand it: what pulled her so strongly toward the stars? Why wouldn't anything else substitute for them?

Amelia's voice lowered to a reverent whisper, and she said, "Has it ever occurred to you that the stars might not be what you're looking for?"

"What?" Sequoia asked, confused. "What else do you think I could be looking for?"

"Humans," Amelia said, and Sequoia had to stop herself from laughing.

The dog just sounded so serious, and she was so completely off-base. Sequoia had never cared two shakes of her tail about humans or what had happened to them.

But clearly, the dog cared. And finally, Sequoia understood

why Amelia had been hanging over her shoulder all week, breathing down her neck, and just generally staying much too close. The dog was hoping beyond hope to get a glimpse of her gods.

Sequoia shook her head, trying to do so as kindly and gently as she could. "No," she said. "No, it's not that."

Amelia smiled condescendingly. "You say that, but how can you know? They're out here somewhere, and even if you're not thinking about them consciously... your spirit may be drawn to them. That's completely understandable. I feel it too. But you know, they don't want to be found, don't you? When we're ready for them, they'll come back to us. The scriptures tell us that. Until then... It's just hubris that keeps us looking, and we're never going to find them. Not until they think we're ready."

Sequoia sighed, suddenly feeling the full weight of her exhaustion settle upon her. Religious dogs made her feel very tired.

Or... wait... was that... gravity?

"Why are we being pulled to the bottom of the ship?" Sequoia asked, trying not to panic as gravity pushed her gently down against her bunk. Sudden sensations of gravity in the middle of empty space could not be a good sign.

Then one of the mouse's voices came over the ship-wide intercom: "Sorry everyone! What you're feeling right now is a side effect of the artificial gravity generator that we engineers— who've been at loose ends all week—have been building in the cargo bay. We didn't realize it would kick into effect as soon as we finished wiring it up, or we would have warned you all!"

Sequoia heard a string of half-hissed, half-growled swear words and other invectives echo down the hallways. It sounded like Captain Kipper had just realized half of her crew had gone rogue and started building dangerously untested devices in the middle of deep space.

Sequoia didn't know if it was the sudden chaos—which reminded her soothingly of being a kit with her parents arguing about nothing much in the other room, knowing they were in charge and would take care of whatever was bothering them—or the gentle press of gravity, but finally, she was able to fall asleep.

CHAPTER 16
KIPPER

ipper knew that it was canonically hard to herd cats, and there were in fact two cats among her engineers... However, she thought that overall it was harder to herd engineers. And as a cat herself, instead of some kind of herd dog, she wasn't at all sure that she was well suited to the task.

The gray tabby grumbled to herself about the difficulty of leadership as she floated through the halls of her ship, mostly as a way to console herself over the fact that she'd missed something as important as three-quarters of her engineering team going rogue and building an untested artificial gravity generator *in deep space*.

You don't build something like that in deep space. You just don't. You need safeguards and safety protocols and backup systems for building something like that.

By the time Kipper arrived in the cargo bay—where the rogue cats, mice, and raptor were clustered cheerfully around a device that looked like the unholy lovechild of a blender, toaster oven, and Klein bottle—her muttered depredations had mostly burned themselves out. All that was left was fire in her eyes and terror in the pit of her stomach.

The mice, cats, and probably raptor (though it was harder to read her feathered face) all grinned at her like kittens with cream dripping from their whiskers.

"Before you say anything," Hedda the head engineer said, floating out in front of the others, "*it works*. You're here, ready to berate us, *because it works*. You felt it."

"We all felt it!" Yvette squeaked, spinning giddily in the restored zero-gee of the spaceship.

"*You could have killed us all.*" Kipper said the words so steadily and so quietly that without the context of the situation, no one could have even told from her tone that she was mad. That's how mad she was. Too mad to even give in to displaying it.

Hedda and Katasha's ears flattened contritely; the mice twisted their long tails in their front paws; and the raptor's feathers fluffed out like a pin cushion.

"We wouldn't have known what went wrong. We wouldn't have even known we were dead, because that's what dead means: you don't know things anymore. And no one back home would have ever known what had happened to us. Just—*poof*—gone." Kipper saw Katasha and several of the mice blanche at that point. They had families who cared about them. Families who'd be devastated if they didn't return.

"I'm sorry," Yvette said, drowning out the muttered apologies from the others. "It was my idea. I should... have asked you."

Kipper kicked a hind paw against the nearest surface, twisting herself away from the gathering of engineers so she wouldn't have to look at her foolish, insubordinate officers while collecting herself. She was too angry to look at them. She wanted to spit and claw and scream.

But.

They had survived.

The moment of most danger was over—turning the device on.

And now she had to deal with the situation in front of her; not the one behind her. Even if she felt like that situation had been handled very, very badly. She couldn't believe she'd been so out of touch with her crew on this tiny little ship that she hadn't noticed three-quarters of her engineers creeping off to the cargo bay to build an artificial gravity generator.

She felt like she was back on *The Jolly Barracuda*, surrounded by reckless, silly otters. Except, she'd never been in charge when she was back there. The responsibility lay at Captain Cod's webbed feet.

Now it was hers, and she didn't like it. She didn't like being in charge. Yet, here she was.

Kipper drew a deep, steadying breath and turned back toward the penitent-looking collection of animals. They knew they had messed up. They'd been gambling with their own lives as much as anyone else's. There was no point in punishing them further than with her disapproval. At least, she'd done that much right: her crew clearly cared about her approval.

"I expect better from each of you," Kipper said through clenched fangs. "Do you understand?"

Every head nodded.

"Now tell me about this—" Kipper waved her paw at the electronic abomination. "—device you've made." It hardly looked big or impressive enough to generate artificial gravity... But then, the pipes which ran throughout the ship, allowing particles to accelerate fast enough to create epsilon jumps didn't actually look like much either.

"It's from the blueprints I brought." Gy'krr spoke in a voice like seagulls calling to the distant sea. Confident, proud, but somehow also a little mournful.

"I thought it would be a good idea," Yvette squeaked. "Most of us engineers didn't have anything else much to do—"

Kipper really regretted not coming up with a task—a safe task—to have kept the engineers busy. That was her fault. Her oversight. And she was damned lucky that it hadn't killed everyone.

"—and I figured, if we at least built the artificial gravity generator, we wouldn't come back to Earth empty-pawed."

Also Kipper's fault: her crew was terrified of coming back to Earth without having found something quasi-magical, something of mythical proportions out here in the galaxy. As if hopping around the galaxy like a doggarned water-skipper on a lake wasn't *good enough*.

"We're collecting amazing data—" Kipper started to say, repeating the party line that she'd been offering Sequoia all week as the squirrel grew more and more anxious. Clearly, the party line wasn't working.

With a deep sigh, Kipper admitted to her wayward engineers, "Look, none of us know what we're doing, and we're all making this up as we go along. But that doesn't mean anyone else— anyone outside our crew—can tell that. We're going to come home heroes to the people who matter—the people who care about progress and science and technological advancement and exploring space. This isn't going to be the end of your careers. I promise. I mean, I may not be able to keep the Uplifted States Space Administration alive, but I'm gonna land on my feet like I always have, and I'll make sure to have positions available for all of you who want them. *As long as we're all still alive and no one blows us up with an untested gravity generator.*"

And just like that, Kipper had looped back around to hissing angrily through her teeth. She could feel the fur under her uniform collar puffing out.

That sudden surge of unexplained gravity had been down-right *scary*. She'd thought they'd been hit by a space rock or fallen into the inescapable orbit of an invisible black hole. She'd thought she'd failed her whole crew, and they were all about to be scrambling for their lives... not that it would help. This far from anywhere habitable, if the ship took damage—real damage, the kind of damage that would feel like a sudden burst of gravity —they'd all be doomed.

It was really hard to shake that fear off and just, you know, act like a reasonable captain in charge of her crew.

But that's what they needed.

They were all staring at her, looking wide-eyed and terrified again. Like they were more afraid of her reprobation than they'd been of the untested gravity generator floating in the middle of the room between them all.

"Okay, right," Kipper said, gesturing at the device again. "So, tell me: how does it work?"

Katasha kicked a striped paw against the wall she was floating beside, pushing herself out in front of the others. The younger cat said, "It's ingenious really. The artificial gravity is generated by a pocket of extra-dimensional vacuum which the device then manipulates into different field shapes based on its settings. Right now, we have the field dialed down so small that you'd have to be inside the device to feel it, and even then, it would be lower than the gravity of a small asteroid."

A couple of the mice chuckled and tittered something about how *they* would fit inside the artificial gravity generator, even if the cats wouldn't. Not that any of them would be foolish enough to climb *inside* the device. No, no, never *that* foolish.

Kipper narrowed her eyes, trying to understand everything Katasha had said. She'd never actually been a scientist or an engineer. She'd been an office temp, handling meaningless paperwork, before she'd somehow found herself a hero astronaut and now captain.

"So... uh... extra-dimensional vacuum? What is that?" Kipper asked, hoping she didn't sound too foolish but also knowing that it was her job sometimes to sound foolish. Sounding foolish was better than being foolish, and pretending to understand something that you actually don't is very, very foolish. Especially on a spaceship. Kipper had learned that the hard way the first time the otter crew of *The Jolly Barracuda* expected her to breathe oxo-agua.

Katasha continued, saying, "An extra-dimensional vacuum is a vacuum that exists in more dimensions than the usual three dimensions of space that we exist in."

Kipper frowned. She thought, but didn't say, "That explanation isn't very helpful." Sometimes, it felt like she had no choice but to be foolish… Maybe it was the universe that was foolish and not her. Because extra-dimensional vacuums sounded very foolish to her, and yet she'd felt the gravitational pull it had caused. "Okay, so, uh, how did you get a pocket of extra-dimensional vacuum?" Kipper pressed.

Hedda answered this time: "We charged the device during the last epsilon jump. Essentially, while the ship was jumping through hyper space, the device was scooping up… uh… the emptiness of those other dimensions we passed through."

Kipper's ears splayed. She couldn't stop them. She tried. It didn't do any good to display her discomfited feelings to her crew, but it also didn't do any good to explain that fact to her ears. They were going to show her emotions right now whether she liked it or not. She was still too rattled by what had felt like her recent brush with death.

And then Trugger swooped into the room like a swirling, swerving, fluffy brown arrow with faded remnants of the green stripes still dyed into his fur. "We are picking up the *weirdest* signal on the bridge," he announced as soon as he'd settled into a still position, with his tail curled around like he was a giant comma.

"What kind of signal?" Kipper asked, her ears perking forward now. Her body was already preparing to brace against death again.

Trugger held out a computer pad, and the engineers crowded around to look at its screen before Kipper could make out anything meaningful.

"That's our extra-dimensional vacuum!" Yvette squeaked.

"Yeah, it sure is," Katasha agreed with the mouse. "It's showing up like a giant red, you-are-here dot on those scans. I wonder..."

Katasha and Yvette looked at each other; mouse and cat with eyes locked together, seemingly thinking the exact same thing.

"What?" Kipper asked. "What are you thinking?"

Katasha gestured to the mouse. "This project was your idea, you say it."

Yvette turned toward her captain and said slowly, seemingly amazed by her own words as she said them, "We can pick up extra-dimensional gravity pockets on our scans, so... maybe if we scan farther afield for them... which we should be able to do, because they exist in hyperspace, unlike radio waves which we have to scan for in real space, and thus are limited by traveling at less than light speed..."

Kipper finally caught up and interrupted: "We might find more pockets of them."

"And that would mean more people generating artificial gravity," Yvette concluded.

"*Humans,*" Katasha muttered, sounding both awed and confused.

"Or octopi," Gy'krr pointed out. "The gravity generator is an octopus technology..."

"Or other, completely alien societies!" Hedda added. The calico cat's golden eyes were practically glowing at the thought. "*Other technologically advanced alien societies.*"

And with that, a look passed between the rest of the engineers, bouncing around between them like a scramball on a game court, until as one, they rushed toward the bridge, shouting and squeaking and meowing and squawking, a riotous ruckus that would wake the antsy squirrel who Kipper had so recently sent away to sleep.

All that was left in the cargo bay was Kipper, Trugger who

looked startled, and the enigmatic appliance that had caused it all.

Kipper glared at the artificial gravity generator for causing so much trouble. Then she gestured to Trugger to follow her and said, "Come on, we need to go keep an eye on them before they do anything else foolish."

"Like hopping us into the middle of a much more technologically advanced and potentially hostile civilization?" Trugger asked.

Kipper shuddered. "Yeah, something exactly like that." She'd never heard Trugger be the voice of reason before. Those ambitious, clever little mice were getting completely out of control. Kipper wasn't sure if she was impressed or terrified. Probably both.

CHAPTER 17
AMELIA

Amelia tried to ignore the racket coming from the rest of the ship, but she feared all the hooting and hollering would wake Sequoia. The squirrel had only just fallen asleep, and she needed her sleep. So, the small dog unstrapped from her bunk, floated over to the door to the barracks, and gently but firmly closed it, blocking out the noise. When she looked back, the squirrel was still sleeping, breathing slowly.

Amelia wondered what all the fuss was about—and also the strange blip of gravity she'd felt a few minutes earlier—but the crew here had proven to be very excitable and unpredictable. If it were really important, Amelia was sure she'd find out eventually.

For now, she found herself entranced by the sight of the sleeping squirrel. Sequoia had been flitting about the bridge, her red brush of a tail flickering like a bonfire on a windy beach, all week long. Her passion for the numbers and graphs representing the stars *The Lucky Boomerang* had visited seemed to rival Amelia's own passion for obeying the dictates of the First Race, and the dog couldn't help but feel there was a connection between those passions.

Sequoia denied it, but Amelia believed the voice the stars

called to the squirrel with was the same voice she heard when she read from the doctrine of the First Race.

In each case, it was the humans who'd uplifted them, calling across the years and light-years to the animals they'd left behind.

Amelia felt sure that if she had enough time with Sequoia, she could help the squirrel find peace—the squirrel would never find the peace she sought by studying the stars or traveling to them. Humans would come home to Earth when they were ready. When the animals they'd left on the Earth were ready. And until then, the peace Sequoia sought among the stars was only truly available in the doctrines of the First Race—religious tomes which explained how dogs were expected to protect and control the other animals of Earth, and how all those animals, together, were expected to wait faithfully for Humanity's return.

Amelia had been putting some thought into which passages of doctrine were the best way to reach a European squirrel who was clearly completely unfamiliar with the intricacies of First Racer theology.

Of course, realistically, when *The Lucky Boomerang* returned to Earth, Amelia would be returning to the Uplifted States to report on the renegade mission, while everyone else from the crew would scatter to the winds—dodging their crimes by returning to Europe or seeking asylum among the otter space stations. But perhaps Amelia could stay in touch with Sequoia. Perhaps as pen pals, she could convert the squirrel to the true way of the world and bring Sequoia the peace that eluded her up here, chasing her tail, ignoring the dictates of what her gods truly wanted from her.

Patience. Loyalty. Devotion.

That's what the First Race wanted from Good Dogs and other uplifted animals. Whereas, the crew of *The Lucky Boomerang* was far too focused on being clever, innovative, and industrious.

That's not what humans had asked of the creatures they'd uplifted—they'd asked for them *to wait*.

Amelia was good at waiting. And it was surprisingly pleasant, floating in the zero gravity of deep space, gazing at the twitchy nose of a beautiful, sleeping squirrel. Amelia wasn't good at reading people—she preferred reading books, especially those that told her she was a Good Dog as long as she waited faithfully for the First Race—but she had become increasingly certain that Sequoia had been flirting with her, and it created a fluttery feeling in her breast that mirrored the way Sequoia's brush of a tail flicked wildly about when new numbers quantifying the stars streamed across a screen in front of her.

Amelia had never been fancied by a squirrel before, and it made her feel almost unaccountably proud. That delicate, frenetic, brilliant but adorably astray creature *fancied her*.

Amelia knew that the First Racers had expected their uplifted animal followers to maintain bloodlines of different breeds who'd been designed over centuries to serve various purposes, working for Humanity. And as such, a relationship between a dog and a squirrel was... well, something of an abomination. However, it wasn't like a dog and squirrel could have children anyway. At least, not as far as Amelia knew. Sure, yes, there was that crazy, deluded dog scientist who had managed to allow dogs and cats to interbreed, leading to horrifying cat-dog hybrids. Were they puppies? Kittens??? No one knew. All Amelia knew was that they shouldn't exist and the doctor behind them was a Bad Dog.

But Amelia was a mutt anyway. Already, a dubious, dead end of the proper genetic lines.

If she happened to develop feelings for a squirrel... and the squirrel requited those feelings... well... if Amelia used those shared feelings to help the squirrel find her way and discover the joy of Waiting Properly for the First Race, then those feelings couldn't really be bad.

Amelia would have to read her books of doctrine over again when she got home. She needed to be sure before proceeding. Before risking an unfaithfulness in her heart, because before all else, Amelia loved the First Race and would do anything to serve them properly. Even accompany this ragtag team of troublemakers as they darted about the universe on their foolhardy errand. Because Dogs were meant to Watch Over the Lesser Animals. And she would do her job.

Because she was a Good Dog.

She would do anything to be a Good Dog.

A small knock sounded on the barracks door, and then the door swung open. Amelia looked over to see one of the mice— the apricot one, Josie—floating in the now open passageway. The doors aboard this ship had all been rigged to open for creatures as small as mice.

"Excuse me," Josie squeaked, "but the Captain sent me. We... uh... we found something, and the captain wants Sequoia to look at it."

"The captain ordered Sequoia to sleep," Amelia woofed softly, trying to avoid waking the squirrel. Though, now that she was asleep, she seemed to be so deeply asleep that she may as well have been dead to the world. "And she's only been sleeping for a few minutes."

"Yes... but..." the mouse began to object, when a second mouse came flying into the barracks, flapping the fabric wings they'd outfitted themselves with. This mouse—the gray one, Yvette—was singing.

"The sky is full of pockets of anti-gravity, hurrah, hurrah! We're going to meet some aliens soon, hooray, hooray! And when we do, I'll be the one who found out you could scan for them, hurrah, hurrah, hooray, hooray, oh joyful, joyous day!"

At the sound of the high-pitched, lilting song, Sequoia quirked one eye half-open, staring skeptically at the world, as though she were gauging whether it were worth actually waking up.

Amelia supposed the answer to that depended on what the squirrel had been dreaming about.

She wondered what squirrels dreamed about.

"Aliens? Anti-gravity?" Sequoia asked groggily.

"We figured out how to generate artificial gravity by scooping up pockets of extra-dimensional vacuum during our epsilon jumps," Josie explained; Yvette was still flapping about the room singing her song. "And then we realized we can scan for similar pockets at a much greater distance than we can search for radio waves."

"Because they exist in hyperspace, which doesn't follow the same rules as our spatial dimensions!" Sequoia's eyes were wide open, and she was unstrapping herself from her bunk now. "And you found some?"

"We found a whole lot!" Yvette answered, breaking off her song mid-verse.

"The captain wants your advice about which of them we should jump toward." Josie might not have been flying circles around the barracks and singing like Yvette was, but the grin beneath her whiskers was so wide it looked almost too big to fit on the face of a mouse.

Amelia's own face twisted in confusion and trepidation. If humans had believed Dogs and the Other Lesser Uplifted Animals were ready for them, they would have simply returned to Earth. They wouldn't have left pockets of extra-dimensional vacuums lying about in space as some sort of ridiculous trail of crumbs to be followed.

So, this couldn't be humans.

But what else could live out among the stars? More barbaric, unruly and ungoverned civilizations like the octopi and raptors of Jupiter? Something utterly alien?

None of that fit within the doctrine of the First Race. And

yet, the octopi and raptors on Jupiter existed, nonetheless, even though the First Race doctrine hadn't warned Earth dogs about how to handle them.

Except, really, First Race doctrine had warned dogs: it had warned them to *wait*. And if they'd waited properly, they'd have never been messing around close enough to Jupiter to find those octopi and raptors.

"I'm not sure this is a good idea..." Amelia found herself speaking to an empty room filled with empty bunks by the end of her sentence. The mice and squirrel were in too much of a hurry to go meet whatever monsters lurked among the stars waiting to harm Bad Dogs who let their wards wander away from where humans had told them to Stay.

Amelia was filled with concern. Whatever these fools had found, it couldn't be good. And it would be her job to protect them from it.

CHAPTER 18
KIPPER

ipper stared at the viewscreen in complete wonder and awe. She had assembled this team, dragged them into the middle of nowhere on a wild goose chase, and yet, there they were: wild geese. The viewscreen was filled with pockets and clusters of pockets of extra-dimensional vacuums (EDV). The scan was overlaid on top of a star map, showing that the vacuum pockets grouped around yellow stars, the exact kind of stars Sequoia had kept *The Lucky Boomerang* chasing after all week.

Not all of the yellow stars were surrounded by the pockets. Most of the yellow stars were single, lonely points of light. Like the stars they'd been jumping between all week.

However, most of the yellow stars with EDV pockets clustered around them wibbled with the characteristic wobble of a star whose light was occasionally blocked by orbiting planets. Kipper supposed that made sense—star systems with planets had more resources and were more likely to foster the development of life or even lure life from other parts of the galaxy. That's why they'd been highest on Sequoia's priority list.

Kipper felt a complicated burst of pride—both in herself for selecting Sequoia as the ship's navigator and even more strongly in Sequoia herself for having been absolutely right about what they should be looking for. It was just that there were so doggarned many stars in the sky. Even knowing what to look for, they could have hopped about from star to star for years without finding anything, so long as they didn't have a map to lead them.

Now they had a map.

They just had to choose which cluster on it looked most promising.

And the person best qualified to make that choice was the hyperactive red squirrel who bounced her way onto the bridge like a fireball special effect in a fantasy movie. She stopped at her post, tail continuing to flutter like a strong wind was stirring the air on the ship's bridge. Her eyes were still red-rimmed from lack of sleep, but her tufted ears stood tall.

Bleary-eyed and bushy-tailed. Exactly what you want from a ship's navigator.

The mice who'd gone to fetch Sequoia—Yvette and Josie— flapped onto the bridge behind her, and Amelia followed them, glaring and grumbling.

"All of these stars have pockets of... uh... what was it? Extra-dimensional vacuum?" Sequoia looked back at the mice, and they both nodded. "It's so many..."

"And so few," Kipper said. "With so many stars in the galaxy, it can be both at the same time."

"Yes," Sequoia agreed. "This is amazing." She stared at the screen with glowing eyes; eyes that mirrored the stars them-selves. "Our galaxy is filled with life."

"And we figured out how to find it!" Yvette squeaked, sounding extremely pleased with herself. The words flirted a thin line with bragging, but Kipper figured the clever little mouse had earned some bragging. Her innovation—and reck-lessness—meant the crew would be less likely to go home empty-pawed.

Although, exactly what they would find among those EDV pockets remained to be seen...

"Not to put too much of a damper on the mood," Trugger said gently, "but we still don't know for sure that those pockets aren't naturally occurring."

Kipper turned to look at her true second in command with quiet shock. This was the second time in a matter of minutes that Trugger had been the one trying to keep her and her crew grounded. She wasn't sure what to make of that, but it didn't seem like a good sign when the otter from *The Jolly Barracuda*—a hotbed of fools and clowns masquerading as pirates—was the one speaking of caution.

"Right," Kipper agreed. "We don't know what we'll find at these stars. We might want to take things slow."

"Slow?" Sequoia asked, blinking. The squirrel looked like she'd never encountered the word or concept of "slow" before in her life.

"Yes," Kipper repeated. "Slow. Can you pick us a star system to investigate that... I don't know... doesn't look threatening? Somewhere we can examine these EDV readings up close without necessarily starting some kind of intergalactic first contact incident?"

"Wait... you want me to pick a star that doesn't seem likely to have much of anyone there?" The squirrel's dainty muzzle gaped open in disbelief.

"That actually sounds like a really good idea," Amelia woofed, looking far less grumbly than when she'd floated onto the bridge after the flapping mice.

The mice, however, now hung in the air beside Sequoia featuring similar expressions of disbelief. "But... but! We found them! Humans or octopi or aliens or something!" Yvette objected. "Shouldn't we go see them?"

"If the First Race had wanted us—" Amelia began to drone

judgmentally, but her words were cut off by a sudden, feline hiss.

Kipper snapped: "Keep your religious nonsense off my bridge! It's enough work figuring out what to do here without some government dog trying to shove First Race doctrine down all our throats."

Amelia's eyes widened, but she kept her muzzle shut. The dog was just smart enough to know better than to try to pull her imaginary rank of second in command. Kipper had left that nonsense behind when she'd cajoled the rest of her crew into committing treason.

"If you aren't committing treason by being here, you don't have a say in this," Kipper mumbled. Clearing her throat, she raised her voice to add, "You are a guest here, Amelia. And if you want to stay on the bridge, you'll keep your muzzle shut unless you have something *helpful* to say, and anything that appears in any book of doctrine of the First Race doesn't count."

Amelia nodded somberly. She kept her mouth shut, and she stayed on the bridge.

Kipper supposed the religious dog felt compelled by her beliefs to stay and monitor the rest of them. As a cat raised in an Uplifted States cattery, Kipper knew just enough about First Racer doctrine to know that Amelia must see herself as some kind of keeper of all the rest of them.

Well, she was welcome to keep on keeping them, as long as she kept quiet and kept her paws and judgmental thoughts to herself.

Kipper looked down at her own paws and realized they were shaking. She couldn't tell how much it was from the stress of command, the terror of what they might find after their next jump, or quixotically from knowing she'd just blasphemed against gods she might be about to meet.

What if they did find humans? And what if Amelia really was supposed to be in charge of them all?

Great gods in the sky, what favors would Kipper be doing for all the cats—and other sentient animals—on Earth if she brought home gods who really did believe that cats were lesser than dogs?

What if the religious dogs were right?

Kipper shuddered.

Pulling herself together, because everyone on the bridge was watching her, Kipper said, "I'm not saying we won't visit one of the dense clusters of EDV pockets. I'm saying we should get our bearings first before jumping into the middle of grand central station, galactic edition."

Katasha, who had been staring at Kipper with awe and admiration ever since she'd snapped at the religious dog to shut up, spoke up to say: "The captain's right. For all we know, these aren't all indicators of technology. Some of them might be singularities—naturally occurring side effects of black holes or some other dangerous natural event. We need to get a closer look from a safe distance."

"Thank you, Katasha," Kipper said. "Now, could we get the engineers back to engineering? The bridge is a bit crowded with all of us in here, and I don't want everyone falling all over each other when we jump."

"You heard the captain!" Trugger announced, beginning to direct the crowd of crewmembers with his paws as if he were a traffic conductor. "Everyone to their posts!"

Most of them willingly followed the otter's directions—engineering cats, dachshunds, and mice streaming out of the bridge entrance and floating or flying down the hall toward engineering. Though, Kipper noticed one of the mice, Yvette, ducked past Trugger, staying on the bridge and taking up a position next to Sequoia, perched on the corner of the squirrel's computer screen. And Amelia took the post that had been hers, by fiat of governmental interference, before all of them—except for her— had committed treason by stealing *The Lucky Boomerang*. It wasn't really her post anymore. But Kipper decided not to press the point.

"And no more messing with that artificial gravity generator UNTIL I SPECIFICALLY SAY SO!" Kipper shouted down the hall after them. It should have gone without saying. But nothing seems to go without saying when you're dealing with an overly clever, ambitious, and bored group of engineers.

When the exodus finished, Kipper looked around at the remaining crew on her bridge—Trugger, Sequoia, Yvette, Amelia, and Gy'krr. The raptor wasn't exactly bridge crew, but she wasn't really an engineer either. Her role onboard—along with her bonded octopus half—was somewhat unclear. A gamble, if you will. Kipper wanted someone—or a pair of some-ones—experienced with raptor and octopus society, and also the massive political shifts that the combined raptor-octopus society had been undergoing. She wanted them onboard in case *The Lucky Boomerang* really did find other societies out here in space. If they did, they'd need every perspective available to them in order to have a chance at bridging a connection. And if these EDV pockets did represent more octopus technology—which they really might, as it turned out octopi were the most ancient and advanced species in the solar system, the only species which had originated elsewhere in the universe—then having represen-tatives from both octopus civilizations in the solar system could prove invaluable.

"Gy'krr," Kipper said, addressing the raptor, "could you go let the octopuses know we're about to jump again? And please bring them back with you to the bridge."

Once the raptor had turned her tail feathers and crawled her way out of the bridge—she was too big to fly in here, even if she did look more like a naturally flying creature than the mice—Kipper turned her attention back to the exhausted squirrel navi-gator who had been stringing herself out all week.

"Have you picked a star system?" Kipper asked gently.

Sequoia pointed at a single star on her screen. Yellow, simple, no wobble that would imply planets, and only a single EDV-pocket. "This one is the least interesting option you could choose," the squirrel intoned drily.

"Perfect." Boring sounded perfect to Kipper. There's nothing quite like being in charge to make a cat become excitement-averse.

As soon as the two octopi and raptor were back on the bridge, settled into their positions, Kipper ordered an epsilon jump, and the way her stomach flipped during the jump was only partly about the ship skipping through folds of hyperspace. It was mostly about what they might find on the other side.

CHAPTER 19
KIPPER

The EDV-pocket orbiting the simple, lonely yellow sun turned out to be contained inside a partly melted lump of metal—a derelict spaceship, abandoned many, many years before, spiraling slowly inward toward the sun. Whoever had been inside the spaceship had escaped, been rescued, or died in there long ago, and the heat radiation from the sun meant there'd be nothing useful the crew of *The Lucky Boomerang* could find inside, even if they were able to tow the vehicle far enough away from the sun to safely examine it.

"It's remarkable that the pocket of extra-dimensional vacuum has survived in there," Sequoia muttered.

Yvette, still perched on the corner of the squirrel's computer station, chittered back, "They're quite stable once they're set up, actually."

"Apparently," Sequoia replied drily. "Can we go somewhere more interesting now?" she asked, turning toward her captain. The glint returned to the squirrel's eye as she pointed a claw delicately at her screen and said, "I've picked out several promising star systems..."

The squirrel's eyes were still bleary.

The government dog was still camped out on the bridge where she arguably didn't belong, arms crossed, and eyes judgmental.

The two octopi continued to gossip in sign language whenever they thought the mammals on the bridge weren't watching —though, now, Nioli was settled into her place on Gy'krr's shoulders, presumably linking their consciousnesses again. Her metamorphic skin had taken on the same tawny, dappled coloring as the raptor's feathers, and the raptor looked much more relaxed now that she was combined with her octopus half again.

Obsidian's skin was the same shiny, inscrutable black as his name. His tentacles—when they weren't busy gossiping—were sprawled over his computer station like an oil slick.

The only animal in the room who Kipper wanted to talk to was Trugger, but she couldn't consult with him in front of the others. The ship suddenly felt far too small, and Kipper felt like the walls of it were closing in on her.

Kipper held up her paws, without thinking, as if she were about to sign something to Trugger, but all the eyes in the room were still on her, and she couldn't bring herself to speak with tongue nor paw. Too much weighed on what she said next.

Fortunately, Trugger knew his captain—and best friend— very well, and he said, "Captain, could I consult with you in private for a minute?"

Kipper swallowed, nodded, and looked about, trying to picture where they could speak privately on this cramped space-ship without fear of being overheard. But Trugger took the matter into his own paws and guided her gently off the bridge and into the central hallway, where he arranged for the two of them to float, facing toward each other and the gaudy, beautiful, oil painting on the wall.

Trugger signed, keeping his paw movements small and

shielded between the two of them, in case any of the rest of the crew tried to follow them, "What's up?"

"I'm sorry," Kipper signed back. "I think..." She shook her head. She didn't know what to say.

"The biggest danger we faced before now," Trugger signed, "was our ship failing—"

"Which didn't worry me," Kipper signed simultaneously to Trugger's signing. "I trust our engineers and the blueprints."

"—and the Uplifted States government trying to throw us all in jail when we get back."

"Also, not a problem," Kipper signed, "if we just never go back."

"But now..." Trugger's paws trailed off into stillness.

"Yes, now," Kipper agreed with her paws. "Everything is different. We might actually find something. Something big. And the last time the two of us headed into dangers unknown, we were almost killed by dinosaurs who should have been dead since before the First Race even existed. I don't want to die. And more than that, I don't want to endanger my crew."

"We could take what we've learned and head home," Trugger suggested. "We've already discovered so much more than we'd expected."

"True..." Kipper's paws stilled. "No, no, we couldn't. I've already taught this crew to commit treason. I think they'd go one step farther and commit mutiny if I tried to take us home without visiting one of those EDV heavy star systems. I don't think they'd even see it as mutiny... just... doing what I was being too cautious to admit I wanted them to do."

Trugger chewed his whiskers thoughtfully, but he didn't contradict her. "I'd have your back," he said.

Kipper didn't really want to start a brawl onboard the bridge as the crew bodily struggled over where the ship should jump next. And she could absolutely picture that happening. She wasn't even sure if she could get away with ordering the crew to take an extra day to study the scans before jumping. She was pretty sure that if she looked away for too long, she'd find her ship epsilon jumping to an EDV-heavy star system without her orders and a whole lot of crew members unwilling to rat each other out about whose paw actually pressed the button.

"Look at it this way," Trugger suggested, "will there ever be a better time or a better crew to take this risk?"

Kipper's eyes narrowed, asking without words for Trugger to explain his meaning.

"If we take this information back home, what do you think will happen?" he asked.

And suddenly Kipper could picture the branching possibilities: governments rushing to beat each other to the punch. President Champ Truman would almost certainly have his dogs commandeer her space program and send a crew of religious zealots. Otters would rush to complete building their own ships based on the ancient octopus blueprints, and based on what Kipper knew of the chaotic way otter society was run, she could absolutely picture Captain Cod blundering his way out of the solar system with his lovable but ridiculous crew before anyone more official could catch up.

Or possibly, a convoy of raptor ships—holdouts from the civil war that had been raging under the clouds of Jupiter— would suddenly resurface, thinking that taking further parts of the galaxy as conquest would give them power again in their home star system.

None of those options were good. They were all troubling in very different ways, but when it came down to it, they were all bad. No matter how much Kipper admired and respected Captain Cod's solid gold heart, she would never put him in charge of a mission this important. And among those options, having Captain Cod stumble into the galaxy like a drunken emu was far and away the best.

"You put this crew together specifically to represent as much of the sentient life in our solar system as possible," Trugger signed. "If there's anything to be found out here, wouldn't you rather that this crew—*your crew*—be the ones to find it?"

Trugger wasn't telling Kipper anything she didn't already know. But he was helping her to clarify it, and she needed to hold that knowledge like a crystal in her heart—clear and bright—if she was going to take this crew—animals who she'd hand-picked and who each trusted her completely, although might still mutiny on her—into an unknown danger.

"Okay," Kipper signed. "Thank you. I guess, I've stalled on this enough."

Trugger's face broke into a huge grin. "There's my cat," he signed.

The two of them re-entered the bridge, and Kipper spoke with both her paws and voice to say, "Finish up collecting readings on the derelict vessel, and prepare for our next jump." Then turning to Sequoia, she added, "Give me your absolute best bet on a star system where..." Her voice caught as she said the next words, having trouble keeping up with her paws, which seemed to feel much less emotional about them: "...humans might have gone."

The tone on the bridge was practically electric—fur puffing up on every animal with fur, including the gray mouse perched on the corner of Sequoia's computer station in obstinate defiance of Kipper's earlier orders for the engineers to get back to engineering. Gy'krr's feathers bristled like a pin-cushion and both octopi began to change colors in rapid, complicated patterns.

Sequoia pointed with a quivering claw at a binary star-system—a yellow star locked in dancing orbit with a smaller white star. "There should be a few planets in this system, possibly habitable," Sequoia said. "But that's not why I think it's our best bet. See this cluster of EDV-pockets?" With a deft motion of her paws, Sequoia zoomed the image in closer. "There's a really big one, with smaller ones close around it, and scattered farther out..."

"You think it's a space station," Kipper said.

Sequoia nodded mutely.

"With spaceships around it."

Another nod.

"And you think it's where humans would have gone?" Kipper pressed.

The squirrel shrugged. "Of all the clusters like it, this one is the closest to Earth. There are other systems with EDV-pockets closer... but they're all smaller."

Kipper caught the sight of motion out of the corner of her eye and looked over to see Obsidian signing with his currently-maroon tentacles, "There may be more individual spaceships, possibly inhabited worlds closer to Earth... But none of them look like *grand central station, galactic edition.* And that's what we're looking for, no?"

Kipper couldn't help quirking a smile at the sight of the octopus quoting her.

"All right, then," Kipper said, feeling like she was jumping off the side of a cliff, or maybe skydiving into a gas giant without the slightest clue what alien horrors might be hiding under its swirling clouds—blimp-like creatures with jagged teeth or maybe clouds of toxic, mind-controlling fungal spores. It could be anything. "Lay in a course for a jump that will take us... to just at the very edge of our sensor range from that cluster of EDV-pockets."

"As measured from the central EDV-pocket or one of the outer ones?" Sequoia asked.

"One of the outer ones, please," Kipper said. It was better to play it safe. "We can always fly closer under the power of normal thrusters once we get there."

"Okay," Sequoia said. "The course is laid in."

Kipper nodded to her, and the squirrel pressed the button, initiating another epsilon jump.

CHAPTER 20
YVETTE

Epsilon jumping through space made Yvette feel like the universe was doing gymnastic flips around her, while she held her own mouse body perfectly still. It was like the inverse of doing gymnastics herself, and it gave her such a sense of stillness and peace. She couldn't tell if she loved the sensation... or if it just felt normal, like the way the universe was always supposed to be, but refused to be until she'd found her way onto this madhouse of a spaceship.

Each time they jumped, Yvette craved the sensation more. Perhaps her true home was up here, among the stars.

CHAPTER 21
SEQUOIA

The *Lucky Boomerang* arrived at the far edge of Sequoia's chosen star system, and suddenly, the viewscreen under her paws lit up like a Christmas tree. The empty vacuum around them became a cacophonous soup of radio waves. The silence of space that she'd grown used to was shattered and gone, replaced with so many signals bouncing in every which direction that looking at them made the squirrel feel like a country mouse who'd arrived in the big city for the first time, dazzled by the tall buildings and neon signs, unsure if she even spoke the local language.

For a moment, Sequoia was thrilled, excitement spiking through her furry body. Then the feeling plummeted, subsumed by something else... something complicated that she hadn't expected.

All of those signals, they meant a thriving interstellar society was nestled around this binary star system like starlings settled on the branches of a big tree. Sequoia didn't want to share her stars with whatever complex society was living here.

She just wanted stars.

Quiet, long-lasting, peaceful, giants floating in the void.

"It looks like we found your *grand central station, galactic edition*, Captain," Sequoia said, almost bitterly. Then she pushed herself away from her work station, floating toward the bridge's door. "Now I'm gonna go get some sleep, just like you wanted me to."

Maybe she would dream about stars.

CHAPTER 22
AMELIA

Amelia's heart jumped inside her chest, and instead of returning to a normal rhythm after the jump, it just kept racing, beating so fast that it felt like it was trying to break free from her body and run toward the humans —her gods!—that she was suddenly certain they'd found.

They shouldn't have been looking.

She was a Bad Dog for being here. A Bad Dog for letting this happen. They were supposed to Wait.

But here they were, and the viewscreen was filled with bright points that—when Trugger zoomed in on them—were clearly artificial structures. Metal objects, strewn everywhere. Space-ships. A space station?

The home of Humanity?

Was this where the First Race had gone?

Were they really Here?

Could a Bad Dog be Rewarded for being Bad?

Or... maybe...

Was this what the First Race had intended all along?

The thought was profound blasphemy, but maybe, the First Race had meant for all the species they'd left behind to work together. Maybe this was what was supposed to happen.

Amelia had spent her whole life being a Good Dog. If this was where her devout behavior had brought her, then maybe she was supposed to be here.

A dark thought occurred to Amelia: maybe none of these spaceships belonged to Humanity. Maybe they'd hopped into the middle of a hive of dangerous wasp-like space aliens who would bring war and devastation to the solar system as soon as they learned of the resources waiting there.

Maybe by being a Good Dog, Amelia would be able to bring warnings of that impending attack back to Earth and all the other Good Dogs there before it was too late.

Maybe she was simply a tool of the First Race and shouldn't worry so much about how they used her.

Maybe she needed to wait until the crew of *The Lucky Boomerang* knew more before jumping to conclusions.

Maybe her faith in the First Race would carry her through, if she could just be a Good Dog and Trust them, rather than worry about the possibility—the shining, glorious, unthinkably wonderful possibility—of getting to meet her gods one day face to face.

Maybe today.

Maybe.

There were too many maybes, and it felt like they were ripping Amelia's curly-furred body apart in every direction. "I think..." Amelia said, "I'm going to retire for now as well." She had no power here. Captain Kipper had made that clear. All she could do was wait until the *cat in charge*—such an oxymoron—chose to bring the ship in closer. And right now, it felt easier to wait in the barracks, near Sequoia, as the squirrel hopefully slept peacefully, than to wait up here, watching the inappropriately powerful cat stumble through making these decisions.

One thing Amelia had to grant about the tabby cat captain—even if a tabby cat should not be a captain—was that she was open and honest with her crew. So, if *The Lucky Boomerang* were to make another, important move, Amelia trusted that Captain Kipper would warn them all.

Until then...

When Amelia reached the barracks, she looked at the red squirrel, fastened in her bunk, bright eyes troubled and pointy ears splayed. Sequoia spread her small arms wide, inviting the curly-furred dog to crawl into her bunk beside her.

Amelia didn't understand the sadness that Sequoia felt about suddenly having to share her stars with an unfamiliar society which had been out here long before her. And Sequoia didn't understand the roiling, tumultuous fervor of Amelia's religious longing to meet humanity.

But they both felt overwhelmed. And tired. And they held each other. And felt safer in each other's arms.

CHAPTER 23
YVETTE

With Sequoia away from the bridge, the squirrel's pilot station was empty—except for the mouse perched on the edge of its computer console. Yvette felt a thrill down to the tip of her tail as she realized that she might be able to take over the station. The cat captain hadn't objected to her staying on the bridge yet. And while messing with the squirrel's computer console might draw attention to her and get her kicked off the bridge and back to engineering, it seemed like a risk worth taking.

There was so much information flashing and streaming over the computer screen beneath her paws!

Yvette wanted to understand it. She wanted to see what was out here among the stars, and from what she'd gleaned of the power structure aboard this ship, staying on the bridge and making herself useful just might lead to an unofficial promotion to bridge crew for her. Captain Kipper seemed to like keeping things unofficial.

So, Yvette busied her paws and mind with trying to make sense of the plethora of information available in this star system. She zoomed in on the visual scans of areas heavy with EDV-pockets and was rewarded with views of spaceships that looked like they'd come right out of the big special effects block-buster movies from Puppywood and Otterwood—gleaming silver rockets; rusty gunmetal gray tanks; copper buckets of bolts. Some of the spaceships looked shiny and new, others looked like they'd survived a war zone. Or maybe—hopefully—just the trials of age.

Goodness, Yvette hoped they hadn't stumbled into the middle of an interstellar war. There were certainly enough different styles of spaceship to support the idea that they repre-sented a whole range of different societies, possibly societies of entirely different species, maybe originating from all different star systems.

But then, Yvette supposed that if she wandered onto a used car lot in Mousfordshire, the different styles, colors, and makes of car might vary almost as much. It's just that she'd be used to them.

Nonetheless, Yvette found herself daydreaming about the different types of aliens who might have chosen to design the different spaceships—one that was all smooth and rounded like a bubble could have been made by fish-like aliens; one built entirely from hexagons and sharp angles could have been built by insectile aliens. Perhaps her daydreams were unlikely, but they were terribly exciting. And right now, in this moment, anything seemed possible. It was exhilarating and made her fur puff out on her neck and shoulders where her uniform didn't hold it down.

While Yvette sifted through all the visuals she could find of spaceships in the binary star system, taking screenshots and cataloguing them for later reference, she heard Kipper and Trugger talking about the radio waves. She looked over and saw that in addition to speaking aloud to each other, the cat captain and otter first mate were both signing back and forth with Obsidian. The octopus, whose skin tone had darkened enough to match his name, was signing back to them with two tentacles while working his console with all six of his others. The appendages slithered and twisted so quickly over his computer console that it looked like a writhing pile of snakes to Yvette. She shuddered. Even though the octopus was her friend, and she'd played countless hands of cards with him, he was still strange to her.

How much stranger might the creatures inside the spaceships she was cataloguing be?

Apparently, Obsidian's acumen for linguistics extended beyond the languages of the living into the languages of the artificial. According to his signing—which Yvette still struggled to keep up with reading—he was a wizard at computer languages, and the captain had him figuring out how to use *The Lucky Boomerang's* computer to convert the various encoded signals bouncing around the binary star system into something understandable.

Yvette paused her own work, cataloguing spaceships, entranced by the idea of seeing what those ships were saying to each other, translated into video that they could actually see.

Obsidian must have been having some luck, because suddenly the main view screen erupted in a chaotic confusion of pixelated colors. Yvette peered at the static, trying to make sense of it. Were there aliens hiding in the colorful storm of pixels? Written language? Anything?

But no, as far as she could tell, it was just static, and everything she imagined seeing there was nothing more than pictures daydreamed in the clouds.

Yvette returned to cataloging spaceships. She'd been working her way clockwise around the biggest cluster of EDV-pockets, spiraling inward. When she got to the middle, Yvette stopped and stared at the structure she saw:

A cluster of several concentric metal wheels, riddled with glowing windows, much, much larger than any of the spaceships around it. In fact, spaceships clung to the outermost ring like bees clinging to honeycomb. It was clearly a space station. The whole thing made her think a little of a gyroscope or a bicycle wheel hanging in the darkness of space between two stars. She wished she could zoom the visual feed in close enough to see through those glowing pinpoint windows, but the resolution simply wasn't high enough at this distance.

"Uh, Captain," Yvette said, still staring at the silver space station. "I think I found Grand Central Station, Galactic Edition for you." She glanced over her shoulder at the cat captain. "Want to take a look?"

"Sure," Captain Kipper said, casually, like she hadn't noticed Yvette had promoted herself to bridge crew without authorization. Or maybe she didn't care, as long as work was getting done. "Put what you've found on the main viewscreen?" Kipper waved a paw at the rainbow storm of pixels currently on the viewscreen. "This clearly isn't ready for us to be looking at it."

Yvette studied the computer station in front of her for a few moments and spotted the controls to share her screen with the bridge's main screen. The buttons were a bit of a reach for her, but she found that the tip of her tail was able to supplement her reach, giving her an additional appendage to work with that the squirrel wouldn't have had. Sequoia's fancy brush of a tail was more decorative than useful.

The silver space station took over the main screen, and everyone on the bridge stared at it. Even Obsidian, who was supposed to be working on the radio signals.

"Are we going to go there?" Yvette asked, her voice small, even for a mouse. She wanted to go there. It was scary, and it could be filled with murderous creatures too alien to ever understand. Or even just more creatures who dwarfed her and could squash her with a misplaced paw like most of the other animals from Earth. But it was also the most exciting thing she'd ever seen in her life.

And then the crackles and sparkles of pixelated static

exploded onto the screen again, replacing the steady, mysterious space station with their chaos. After only a moment, lines formed out of the pixels, and then shapes. The whole image resolved quite suddenly into a scene—both simple and spectacular all at once.

A figure reclined in a chair; another figure paced back and forth in front of the first one, waving a vaguely tentacle-like appendage. Accompanying the scene, the speakers on the bridge blared with indistinguishable noises, causing Yvette to clamp her paws tightly over her large, round ears, pressing them down against her head. Fortunately, the volume dropped quickly, bringing the abrasive sounds into a tolerable range.

"What is this?" Trugger said with voice and paws.

Obsidian waved his own tentacles, answering with signs that moved too rapidly for Yvette to understand all of them. But the gist seemed to involve words centered around "translate" and "program" or "message."

"So... it's like, what, an alien sitcom?" Trugger asked, tilting his head to the side, staring at the screen.

Yvette did the same, unconsciously mimicking the otter's head tilt as she narrowed her eyes, focusing on the two figures' faces, trying to make sense of them. The one waving a tentacle-limb around also had tentacles for a face, which made it even weirder looking than Obsidian and Nioli. It could have been a Cthulu-monster from some ancient human horror flick. The one sitting in the chair looked... well... approximately like a giant bee, except its stripes were royal purple and evergreen. Yvette couldn't help wondering if the spaceship with all those hexagons in its design was associated with the green-and-purple bee's species.

"Or it's an alien news program," Captain Kipper suggested. "Do you think you'll be able to translate what they're saying?" she signed to Obsidian.

The octopus's yellow eyes flitted between the image on the

screen and the tabby cat captain. Then he twisted a single tentacle into the sign for "yes," followed by something that seemed to amount to, "with enough time and video to study."

"Is there enough video to study?" Kipper asked.

Obsidian's tentacles flew over his computer console, tangling and twisting, changing color from the dark shade they'd taken on, fading to almost white. Then brightening to a ruddy shade of mauve. As Obsidian's color changed, so did the view on the main viewscreen—images flitted by dizzyingly, too quickly for Yvette to completely make sense of them, but it looked like more aliens, more different kinds of aliens, all kinds of aliens. Too many aliens. This had to be some sort of collection of sci-fi movies from space with all kinds of fictional beings, all imagined up by just a single species or two. Clearly, some overly creative otters had left the solar system behind and hidden out a couple hundred light years away, busily animating futuristic sci-fi films. That made more sense than what Yvette was seeing.

And yet, she'd seen the spaceships too.

She'd already wondered about how many different species of aliens it might take to design that many different kinds of space-ships. Maybe it was a lot.

Maybe the universe was a lot more crowded than anyone back on Earth had realized.

The viewscreen returned to the stable, steady view of the gyroscopic space station, and Obsidian signed with pale pink tentacles, slowly and clearly, "There's more than enough video to work with. I don't know how much time I need. It depends on how many different languages they're using."

CHAPTER 24
SEQUOIA

Sequoia woke up from a sleep so deep that it was as if she'd disappeared from the universe for a while, blinked out of existence into an entirely separate realm of blissful unconsciousness.

The universe she woke up into felt like an alternate reality. Sure, she'd been the first one to flirt with Amelia by braiding the curly fur on the dog's face, and she'd been the first one to fall asleep in the dog's bed, innocently sharing a pillow... But now, she'd woken up with her red-furred arms tangled up with the mop dog's blonde curls, and the dog's arms wrapped tightly around her. It was more. It was different. It felt like the beginning of something and not just a playful flirtation. They'd come to each other when tired and overwhelmed. They'd turned toward each other like orbiting stars, like they were held together by each other's gravity. Like they were building a relationship.

But more than that, sounds echoed through the halls of the ship that made no sense in Sequoia's pointed ears. For a moment, they'd sound like conversation, but she couldn't make out any of the words. Then the rhythms would change in unexpected ways, screeching or singing or warbling... Sequoia wasn't sure. It didn't sound like anything she'd ever heard before.

Next to Sequoia, the blonde mop of a dog opened her brown eyes, which were still beautiful, kind-looking, and soulful, framed by the delicate little braids which were coming apart in charming wisps after a week of wear.

Amelia looked startled for a moment, but she didn't push Sequoia away. Instead, she sighed, deeply, and squeezed the squirrel tighter. But then her floppy ears perked up, as much as floppy ears can, and she asked, "What is... that?"

"I don't know." Sequoia shook her head. "I don't feel like I know anything any more." She was thinking about her stars and how they'd gone from being pristine, perfect balls of fire, spinning through the universe as its sole inhabitants, to becoming nothing more than a backdrop to those eerie EDV-pockets that had popped up everywhere as soon as the mice had figured out to look for them.

Sequoia pushed gently against the rumpled, navy blue cloth of Amelia's uniform, gaining enough space between the two of them to begin unharnessing herself from the cot. Without the dog's arms or the harness holding her down, she immediately began floating away. "I don't know what those sounds are, but I'm going to go find some breakfast, and then maybe I'll have the strength to face... whatever that is."

"That's a good idea," Amelia agreed, smoothing her uniform down and unharnessing herself as well.

The squirrel and dog dug into the stash of granola bars stored in a cupboard between the cots. It wasn't an exciting breakfast, but then, none of the food in space had been exciting after the feast with all the otters on Europa. Mostly, food in space has to be a practical matter—nothing with too many crumbs or droplets or bits that can get away; nothing that needs complicated cooking; nothing that doesn't store easily.

Maybe it was different on otter spaceships. Sequoia didn't

know for sure… Although, Trugger had certainly told tales about the delicacies cooked up by Emily, the octopus chef, on *The Jolly Barracuda*. But for now, the Uplifted States space program was still in its infancy—still enduring the early days of simple rations.

The granola bar suited Sequoia well enough with its crunchy clusters of nuts, simultaneously salty and sweet. Amelia supplemented her granola bar with a chewy looking piece of beef jerky. They ate in silence. Well, *they* stayed silent. The strange, confusing sounds continued to echo through the rest of the spaceship, leaking into the barracks like an audio-only window on another universe.

"I keep thinking I'm starting to make sense out of these sounds…" Sequoia carefully folded up the foil wrapper from her granola bar and stashed it into the waste bin at the bottom of the cupboard while warbles and wails continued to assault her pointed ears. "But I'm not. I have no clue what these sounds are, and I think it's starting to drive me mad like some god of cosmic horror from a really artsy film student attempt at a sci-fi movie."

Amelia laughed. She folded the wrappers from her breakfast just as carefully as Sequoia had before stashing them in the waste bin as well. Sequoia smiled at that. She didn't really understand the feelings her heart insisted it was having for this dog. But there wasn't anything much she seemed to be able to do about them, so she might as well enjoy watching Amelia be cute and fastidious.

"Okay, time to be a flying squirrel," Sequoia said, kicking off from the closest bunk and gliding toward the hallway out of the barracks. She heard a scuffling of claws behind her that suggested Amelia was following. The two of them made it out into the hall and floated, staring at each other, and twisting their ears experimentally. "It's coming from both the bridge and the engine room, isn't it?"

Amelia nodded. "Shall we try the engine room first? The sound seems to be louder from there."

Sequoia's post was on the bridge. But she didn't feel like going back there. She'd spent so much time over the last week at that post hoping and grasping... and then she'd grabbed hold of more than she'd meant to, and her paws had been burnt. It was all exhausting and overwhelming. Much like these bizarre sounds, causing her ears to twitch and twist and flatten. "Sure, engine room first," Sequoia agreed. For her, she mostly associated the engine room with pleasant, friendly games of poker with the mice and Obsidian. She kicked off the nearest wall and took off flying through the hallway.

When they arrived at the engine room, all of the engineers—cats, dogs, and mice—were huddled in front of the bank of video screens that usually showed external views of the ship, internal views of the hardest-to-reach and most important parts of the ship's internal machinery, and readouts of the engine's status.

Right now? Those screens were filled with bizarre scenes of disparate alien figures who looked like they'd been pulled right out of a lineup of summer blockbuster sci-fi films—spiders, fish, tentacled things, gleaming silver robots, and fuzzy people of every color, shape, and size.

"What the hell?" Sequoia asked. "What are all these videos?"

The engineers didn't even turn to look at her, but the gray mouse, Yvette, shushed the newcomers to the engine room vigorously. *"It's local video feeds we've picked up. We're trying to learn the languages in them,"* she hissed in a whispered rush, clearly trying not to interrupt the cacophony of sounds accompanying the screens.

"Or learn anything about them, really," another mouse volunteered. The orange one, Josie.

"Oh my goodness, you're eating popcorn?" Sequoia asked, recognizing a few of the characteristically puffy kernels floating among the viewers. They had a bowl with a catch-top designed to let paws reach in for popcorn while keeping most of it inside, but a few stray kernels had escaped.

"Hey, this is the best movie night I've ever been to," another mouse squeaked. It was Mulberry, with the Siamese points to her coloring. She had a kernel of popcorn cradled in her paws that was almost as big as her head. The tooth marks on it suggested she'd been nibbling it for a while. "We've been watching these videos for *hours*. It's better than being back in college and procrastinating studying for finals."

All three of the other mice shushed Mulberry.

"Oh come on, guys," said Katasha, the cat with coloring to match Mulberry's. "It's not like any of us are actually cracking the code of lingua galactica here."

"That's Obsidian's job," Hedda mumbled. The calico engineer pulled a pawful of popcorn out of the bowl without taking her eyes off the screens.

Katasha pointed a paw at one screen and said, "We think this one's a news show." Her pointing claw changed angles, moving one screen over. "This one seems to be some kind of sitcom." Her paw continued to move down the bank of screens as she said, "We have no idea what in the hell is going on here; we're hoping to hell that this one is a movie or something else wildly fictional, because if it's not, we should fly home with our tails tucked between our legs and hide on Earth for the rest of our lives, like, *yesterday*."

"No kidding," Hedda agreed.

Freddy the dachshund laughed and said, "What, you don't think being in the middle of an intergalactic war would be fun?"

All of the mice squeaked "No!" in a surprisingly harmonically pleasing chorus.

"How can you stand listening to all of those at once?" Sequoia asked in wonder. She felt like stuffing her ears full of cotton to make the noises stop.

Katasha shrugged. "You get used to it."

"And when you have information like this available..." Yvette trailed off, staring at the screens. The gray mouse was twisting her tail in her paws, and her eyes were so bright they could have been tiny stars all of their own. "You want to absorb as much of it as possible, as fast as possible."

Sequoia worried about the fact that none of them had been echoing their spoken words by signing with their paws—their paws were mostly too busy with popcorn—but a glance at Georgie showed that the larger dachshund was so deeply absorbed in staring at the bank of screens that he wouldn't have seen any signing done for his benefit anyway. She wondered if the videos were more or less disturbing without the overlapping gibberish of noise accompanying them. She had to suspect that this particular experience would be strictly better without sound. If she could mute all the videos without a host of engineers attacking her, Sequoia would do it right away.

Instead, the squirrel settled for turning tail and heading toward the bridge to see if the situation was more informative and less overwhelming there. She reached the door to the hall and looked back to see that Amelia wasn't following her.

The curly-furred dog was staring dumbstruck at the screens, and Sequoia was about to write her off as having joined the host of mesmerized engineers when a certain glimmer in Amelia's eyes stopped her short. She tried to follow the dog's gaze to exactly which screen had captured her attention and saw something she hadn't expected:

A figure with long hair growing from the top of its head, flowing down its shoulders, and framing an oval face of naked, furless skin. A primate. But not just any primate.

Sequoia had seen ancient human movies before. She'd seen statues. She knew what humans looked like.

This was a human. Unmistakably so.

No wonder Amelia was transfixed.

Sequoia kicked off the hallway door to get some momentum

and floated back to the group. She said, "Hey, isn't that a human?" She pointed at the screen which had frozen Amelia as still as a statue herself.

"Sure seems to be," Freddy agreed. "They've been showing up periodically in a number of the video feeds." He didn't seem too concerned. Not like Amelia.

A strangled squeak escaped Amelia's throat, but she still didn't move. Her eyes didn't even waver from staring at the one human face, until the scene changed and the human went away. Then Amelia gasped, as if the spell holding her had been broken. She turned her face away from the screens and flailed her paws, awkwardly careening out of the engine room, as fast as she could. As if she were running from a fire.

Sequoia followed Amelia back to the barracks at a much more reasonable speed and arrived to find the dog floating in the middle of the room like a windup toy whose spring had wound down.

"Are you okay?" Sequoia asked.

Amelia shook her head; everything about her seemed to be quivering. She was so tough and self-possessed most of the time. Ready to boss everyone on the ship around, even the captain. But now, it was like she'd seen a ghost.

Or her god.

"I mean... you've seen humans before, right?" Sequoia asked. "Like ancient movies? Right?" If squirrels watched ancient human movies, then it seemed like dogs—who worshipped humans—*must* watch them too. But maybe they didn't. Maybe they thought it was blasphemy of some sort. Dogs seemed to be big on the concept of blasphemy and using it as an excuse to ban perfectly good things from what Sequoia had been learning about the way they ran the Uplifted States.

"Yes," Amelia said softly. "I've seen human movies. Watched human television shows. Appreciated human paintings. Read human books. I've spent my whole life studying them and the clues they left behind for us, just as any Good Dog does."

"But this is different?" Sequoia prompted when it became clear that Amelia didn't intend to say anything more.

"This is different," Amelia agreed. "Those... everything we have... it's ancient. It comes from lifetimes before I was born. But that video..."

"We don't know how old it is," Sequoia pointed out.

"True, we don't." But Amelia's eyes didn't look any less haunted.

Sequoia didn't know what to say, so she waited.

Eventually, Amelia said in slow, measured tones, "I knew they were out here. I never doubted they were out here. But..." Her voice choked before she managed to continue. "To look at your God when they haven't asked you to... To break their Command and Follow them when you weren't Asked... weren't Wanted..."

"How do you know you're not wanted?" Sequoia asked.

"They told us to Stay," Amelia whispered.

Sequoia didn't know anything about First Racer doctrine. But she wanted to make her friend—possibly girlfriend—feel better. "Didn't they also tell you to... uh... look out for the other animals on Earth?"

"Yes."

"Well, no one told me to stay," Sequoia said. "And I've heard voices calling me to the stars my whole life, so you were never going to stop me from coming out here. Maybe... maybe you just did what you had to do. Maybe that's what they would have wanted from you. Maybe... maybe you'll be able to ask them?"

"*Ask them if I was a Good Dog?*" The whisper was so quiet, it was barely more than a breath, shaped into all of Amelia's hopes.

"I guess," Sequoia agreed. Though, she was troubled by the

idea that so much of Amelia's—or anyone's—sense of self-worth would depend on what a virtual alien had to say to them.

Because even if there were humans out here, and they had come from Earth... They weren't part of Earth anymore. They hadn't been for a long time.

CHAPTER 25
KIPPER

Kipper was struggling really hard to make a decision that she knew would be unpopular with her crew when Amelia burst back onto the bridge, zooming like a fuzzy meteor, followed more sedately by Sequoia. The squirrel looked much better rested now. That was good. Amelia looked... half-crazed. There was a glittering gleam in her brown eyes that worried Kipper... but somehow felt inspiring too? Like Amelia was one of those preacher dogs who could get a whole church dancing on their paws and howling like feral wolves, overflowing with a frenzied, communal joy.

"You have to let me come with you," Amelia said. "I need to be one of the crew members who actually steps paw on the space station. And you need me with you."

Kipper frowned but didn't say anything. Clearly, Amelia didn't know that her captain had been moments away from announcing that *The Lucky Boomerang* had gathered enough data, and it was time to fly home, still safe, still alive, and heroes. Let the dogs back home argue about how to proceed with actually contacting this interstellar soup of civilization that they'd successfully managed to blunder into out here. Let someone else lead the mission of first contact. Kipper had done enough, and it was time to go home.

Kipper had found more than she'd been looking for—more than she could have imagined out here. According to Obsidian, most of the video programs that the engineers were busy watching were part of a bundle of data that streamed between a fair number of the vessels out here—something like interstellar cable, Kipper supposed. But the octopus had also found a lot of shorter bursts of data and seemed confident that they were actual real-time communications between the various starships and the space station they were all swarming around.

If Obsidian was right, and he'd successfully managed to intercept videos showing who was actually aboard these spaceships, then they'd stumbled into a neighborhood with dozens of different alien races, what seemed to be sentient robots, and of course, the one that was most familiar and yet also most mythical of all: humans. Actual humans.

Kipper had travelled out into space and found her second grade teacher's gods. And her dentist's. And most of the politicians running her country. Kipper had known so many dogs— and even a few cats over the years—who worshipped humans. And Kipper had never thought very hard about them. Sure, she'd used the specter of finding humans as a rationale for the space program she believed in so deeply... but she'd been using a popular idea that she knew would appeal to the dogs with money and the power to say 'yes' to her project. She hadn't really thought she'd find them. Maybe... some ruins? Some abandoned, derelict space vessels? Maybe some clues?

But... living humans?

Kipper didn't think they were gods. And yet, they had engineered her people, redesigning their bodies from four-legged, feral things—beasts with feelings, but no words—into full people who could talk and write and make art and design technology of their own.

Kipper had to admire that. She had to feel grateful for it. Deep inside herself, she felt the pull of that power. These were the people who had made her. She wanted to believe they'd be pleased with and proud of what she'd become, what she'd made of the gifts they'd given her, and yet Kipper knew that made no sense at all. Whatever people—whatever human beings—she might meet on that space station had had no hand in her lineage. They were great, great, great, great-grandchildren at best of the humans who'd actually lived on Earth.

Would they even know what to do with her?

Would Kipper know what to do with them?

Kipper raised a paw to silence Amelia's continuing pleas and explanations of how useful she'd be on a mission to actually meet the humans. Most of her arguments seemed to boil down to her having greater experience with diplomacy and deeper knowledge of human history than anyone else onboard. Kipper wasn't sure the former was true, given the work Nioli and Gy'krr had done during the octopus revolution on Jupiter, and the latter? Human history wouldn't help here.

Understanding human history wouldn't be any more useful for understanding the interstellar society in front of them than understanding a feral, pre-uplift cat would be for understanding Kipper's brilliant, erratic sister Petra. Furthermore, being a devout First Racer meant Amelia was profoundly emotionally compromised when it came to the question of possibly actually making contact with the aliens—and humans—out here.

And yet, Amelia would be Kipper's most direct liaison to the Uplifted States government—the government in charge of her space program—when they got home.

Kipper needed Amelia happy with her if she wanted any chance of salvaging her position running the USSA when they returned to Earth, rather than just automatically planning on defecting back to the chaotic society of otters in the sky.

"I haven't decided whether we're actually going to approach

the space station," Kipper admitted to the frenzied dog in front of her. She saw a stillness form in the other members of her crew on the bridge—even Trugger—as they heard her words as well.

They had all been assuming, without the slightest question, that if you find a space station swarming with spaceships in the depths of space, buzzing with video feeds that seem to show a wide range of arts and entertainment, implying some kind of a civilized culture... you, *of course*, approach it. You fly up and say, "Hello."

Kipper wasn't so sure. They had enough data available to study it for a long time, and wasn't it safer to wait until they understood what they were seeing in all these video feeds? Wouldn't it be better to send a crew of trained diplomats?

Of course, was there really such a thing as diplomat trained for this situation?

And wasn't that exactly why Kipper had picked representatives of all the major species in the solar system for her crew, including a bonded octopus and raptor pair who had just navigated the complete overhaul of their society through revolution?

Amelia's eyes still looked wild with desperation and clawing need, so it was kind of unsettling when she spoke in a completely calm voice: "We will return heroes from this mission, even if we turn around and head home now. All of us. But there are Humans on that space station, and when President Truman and the rest of the government at home get wind of that, what do you think is going to happen to your space program?"

No one answered. The two octopuses, raptor, and Trugger all looked to Kipper. She knew the answer, but she didn't want to say it.

"What will happen?" Trugger finally asked. For all the time he'd spent with Kipper, he really wasn't well-versed in Earthly politics.

Bleakly, Kipper said, "We'll all be heroes, but we'll never set paw in this spaceship again. The next crew will be entirely dogs. Devout, devoted, fervent First Racer dogs. And not one of us will set paw near space via this space program again until... I don't know. I genuinely don't know what all those religious dogs will do about the humans out here, but I do know that they won't let a single cat—or any other species, even including non-religious dogs—have any part of it, not until they feel it's settled."

Amelia nodded. And Kipper realized, Amelia's impassioned plea was because the dog knew she wouldn't be a high enough ranking dog to be sent on that second mission. She'd be locked out of meeting the humans on that space station as absolutely and completely as everyone else currently aboard *The Lucky Boomerang*. If Amelia was low-ranking enough to be sent along as a babysitter on this mission, she definitely wouldn't rank high enough for *that* mission. This was possibly her only chance to meet her own gods face to face.

Kipper wanted to play it safe, but sometimes playing it safe meant willingly relegating yourself to the sidelines. And being a hero wasn't good enough for Kipper if all it meant was being a figurehead. Kipper wanted—*needed*—to be involved in setting policy. Because she was never letting those religious dogs back home landlock her or any other cat, anchoring their paws to the surface of the Earth.

"You can come," Kipper said to Amelia. She would bring one member, at least, of each species aboard *The Lucky Boomerang* who wanted to come. Each species deserved representation. Of course, that was getting ahead of herself. First, they had to wrangle an invitation. Kipper turned to her octopus translator, Obsidian, and signed, "Have you figured out what kind of message we could send to that space station to let it know we'd like to dock with it?"

Obsidian's pale pink tentacles fluttered in a rapid answer:

"I've isolated a lot of patterns from the communications between the vessels and the central space station. And yes, one of them does seem to be a request to dock, which I could easily copy and transmit."

With far too much portent weighing on her shoulders, Kipper signed back, "Send the message."

Only moments later, Obsidian reported that they'd received in return what seemed to be an automated response, inviting them to dock and directing them to a particular docking berth.

The joy that filled Amelia's eyes troubled Kipper.

CHAPTER 26
YVETTE

While Sequoia piloted *The Lucky Boomerang* toward the mysterious, exciting space station, all of the engineers gathered around the deck of poker cards in engineering, breathless to find out which one of the mice would get to join the away mission. The slots for cat and dog were already filled by Captain Kipper and Amelia.

Hedda shuffled the deck, and the four mice drew cards, nearly as large as themselves—high card wins—to decide which one of them would get to represent all of mouse-kind.

Yvette won with the queen of spades, and it felt like the first time she'd shot the moon while playing hearts as a tiny mouse pup just learning the game. It felt better than any of the bronze or silver medals she'd ever won at gymnastics competitions, because it didn't come with as much baggage and uncertainty—had she performed well? Could she have performed better? What would the medal mean for her future career prospects?

This was based on pure randomness—what order the cards happened to be in when she drew from the deck—and the reward was simple, straightforward, and so much more exciting than anything that any mouse on Earth had ever won.

Yvette had won an opportunity to see something marvelous that no other mouse had ever seen.

And yet, as she watched the whiskers droop on Josie, Mulberry, and Wendall's faces, even this euphoric high became something mixed. It wasn't a happiness that she could share, and that made it much less sweet.

Quickly, Yvette fixed the natural grin that had raised her whiskers, contorting her muzzle into an expression of glee—she toned her external enjoyment down several notches. Trying to find an appropriate amount to be happy. An amount that wouldn't make her friends unhappy with her.

Josie smiled, reached out a paw, took hold of Yvette's paw and squeezed. "You'll tell us all about it."

"I will, of course," Yvette agreed, almost too eagerly, hoping to make up for winning this opportunity—and thus denying it to the others—by trying to share vicariously.

The more that Yvette lived, the more she was coming to think it wasn't losing she disliked—it was competition itself. She wanted everyone to be able to win. All together. Like when they'd built the artificial gravity generator, and it had been one big group project with everyone participating.

Unfortunately, in this case, the captain was in charge, and Captain Kipper had been clear that she didn't want the mission crew to get unmanageably large. (Not that a couple extra mice would add much size... but, they might add a lot of complication.)

Yvette and the other engineers—none of whom would be joining the away mission, since Kipper would be representing cats and Amelia dogs—watched the spinning, silver space station grow larger on the viewscreens in engineering as *The Lucky Boomerang* approached. Bands and boxes of brightness lit up the silver wheels of the space station—long windows, showing the light inside. The video feed was, of course, being recorded, but Katasha scribbled pencil sketches in an actual notebook, trying to capture the images of every spaceship they passed, including little notes about how they might be structured internally. That cat was a spaceship engineer to the core.

Hedda and the dachshunds just watched the screens in awe, shifting their positions to match their shifting weight as *The Lucky Boomerang* synchronized its momentum with the spinning wheel of the space station. All four mice had clustered on one of the control panels together with Yvette in the middle, holding each others' paws and twining their tails into a tangled braid as if they were a tiny rat king of legend. Yvette felt like the other three were trying to absorb as much of her presence as possible, as if by doing so they could haunt her and somehow accompany her on the upcoming mission, spiritually if not physically.

As *The Lucky Boomerang* slowed to barely moving, floating within kissing distance of the space station, the calico cat engineer began swearing under her whiskers. "Holy hell, they have mutable metal." She pointed at the screen showing an external view of *The Lucky Boomerang's* own airlock, where the space station's docking clamps had reached out and were melding themselves into the right shape to lock securely onto the ship's exterior. "If we want to break away from here without permission, we'll tear our own airlock off. I hope to hell the captain knows what she's doing."

Katasha laughed, a uniquely feline sound with its touch of a purr. "You know she doesn't. None of us know what we're doing anymore."

"We're doing what we have to," Georgie signed, seemingly having read Katasha's muzzle as she spoke. The Siamese tabby tucked her ears in apology at not having signed to make it easier for the deaf dachshund to understand her. "That's what we're all doing out here—what we have to."

Georgie and Freddy had explained to the rest of the engineers earlier what would happen if *The Lucky Boomerang* brought back news of humans without having made actual contact with them: the whole Uplifted States space program would get locked down, bogged down by religious dogs, inaccessible to anyone but the most devout canines.

Maybe some otters would be spurred by the information that *The Lucky Boomerang* returned with to build their own interstellar vessels, or perhaps try to retrofit existing spaceships with epsilon drives. But they'd be months behind *The Lucky Boomerang* at best. Basically, first contact would belong to the First Racers.

No one onboard, even Amelia it seemed, wanted that. It was better to take the leap and make first contact themselves, even if that meant letting this foreign space station lock itself to their airlock, leaving them with no easy escape from the unknown.

Except, the society aboard that space station wasn't entirely unknown. The mice and everyone else aboard had been watching hours upon hours of the media that this interstellar society spilled into the vacuum of space, and while they actually understood very little of it... Some of it was clear: there were creatures and beings of all different sorts out here among the stars, and they interacted with each other. They stood in rooms together and made sounds at each other like they were speaking; they built spaceships that could protect them from the harsh vacuum of space, and they congregated together.

Some of that had to be good.

Some of that was much like what *The Lucky Boomerang* looked like, except on a much, much bigger scale. A grander scale. A galactic scale.

Yvette got shivers down her spine, puffing out her fur, just thinking about it. She felt small being a mouse on a spaceship built for cats and dogs, but she felt even smaller thinking about what they might find on the space station they were about to board.

"Alright, we're docked," Hedda said, and the shifting gravity caused by the ship's centripetal motion had indeed settled down to a normal-feeling downward pull. It felt like a perfect approximation of Earth's gravity. Hedda's feline face with its lopsided calico markings melted into a beatific smile, and she announced, "Let's get our representative engineer to the airlock."

All of the engineers looked happy for Yvette—the dachshunds' tails wagged; Katasha purred; and the other three mice were practically jumping for joy. Apparently, there wasn't room left over for jealousy with how much excitement filled and overflowed in them all.

Yvette may have been the only engineer invited on the away mission, but this was still a triumph for all of them. They'd built and flown a spaceship across hundreds of lightyears, and now they would take their first steps into joining an interstellar community where the entire solar system altogether only added up to one small drop.

Georgie offered his paw to the cluster of mice, making it a ramp to his shoulders. Yvette climbed up and settled beside one floppy, brown ear. She flapped her fabric wings as Georgie walked down the hall, carrying her, as if she were still flying like a tiny bird. The other engineers followed in a crowd, each cat and dog with a mouse on their shoulder. The mice could no longer fly using their cloth wings, now that *The Lucky Boomerang* shared in the space station's gravity.

Yvette flipped her long tail in complicated curlicues, enjoying the ride on Georgie's shoulder and the anticipation of the unknown to come. When they made it to the airlock, Captain Kipper, Trugger, Amelia, and the bonded pair of Nioli and Gy'krr were already suited up and standing in the airlock. Inside their conjoined spacesuit, with Nioli settled on Gy'krr's shoulders, the two of them looked like a magnificent creature—strong legs, two arms, and eight tentacles sprouting from the raptor's back like frightening, angelic wings. Yvette could see why—if the two of them truly enjoyed and complimented each other—they wouldn't want to give that joint existence up.

"Nioli is the octopus on the mission?" Katasha asked with

characteristic catly curiosity. "Not Obsidian? I thought he was specifically here for his facility with languages and translation."

Captain Kipper answered, "Obsidian feels he'll be able to concentrate better in familiar surroundings. He'll be observing the audio-video feeds from our suits and transmitting back real-time attempts at text translation. You are, of course, all welcome to watch our video feeds as well."

"Oh, we will be," Hedda declared. "Eagerly."

"Fervently," Katasha added.

The three mice who would be staying aboard *The Lucky Boomerang* said nothing, but Trugger leaned conspiratorially toward Josie, sitting on Katasha's shoulder, nonetheless and offered, "I could sneak you on the mission inside my space helmet if you'd like. I think you'd fit."

"I heard that," Captain Kipper declared dryly, seemingly unbothered by her first officer pretending to undermine her orders.

Trugger shrugged. "Well, I had to try. Maybe I'll be able to bring you all back some souvenirs!"

"No squirrel?" Freddy asked, looking around the gathered crew. "Sequoia isn't joining you?"

"She declined my invitation," Captain Kipper said. "But I think we have enough of the solar system represented here, and most likely, this won't be our last foray into interstellar society."

Yvette finished securing her own spacesuit and hopped onto Trugger's shoulder. The otter, conjoined octopus-raptor, officious dog, and cat captain all crowded into the airlock together. The inner door to the airlock closed. The air began to cycle out —Captain Kipper didn't want to waste any of the ship's precious air if there turned out to be anything wrong with the air on the space station. And once the group of them stood in a small patch of vacuum, Trugger stepped forward, saying, "Where skylarks roam..." and pressed the controls to open the outer door.

Yvette drew a breath sharply through her whiskers as the metal airlock spiraled open, revealing a bustling scene.

The docking hangar on the space station yawned out in front of them with massively high ceilings, a distant far wall with many windows and doors in it and the sides curving into the distance with no visible end. The ceiling and far wall curved as well; the whole space was part of a spinning ring, which *The Lucky Boomerang* had attached to the side of, and through the many windows in the ceiling, Yvette could see more rings, the inner rings of the space station above.

In the yawning space around them, alien creatures of all sorts—large and small, furry and scaly, feathered and leafy, and some too strange to understand—wandered and gathered, stacked boxes and crates of cargo, and pushed cargo about on floating dollies. A lot of the aliens looked vaguely canine, many with red fur and pointy ears. Yvette supposed she shouldn't be surprised to see that dogs—or dog-like creatures—were prevalent even out here in deep space. Dogs were so good at feeling like they belonged anywhere they happened to be that, of course, they would have evolved on other worlds as well.

A few of the creatures moving through the crowds among the docking berths were clearly human, living versions of the statues Yvette had seen back home. And even though mice had no religions built up around humanity, the sight of them made Yvette's fur prickle under her uniform. Seeing living humans felt like seeing unicorns or gryphons—something Yvette had never imagined she would see except on a video screen, fictional and fabricated, conjured by the clever work of an artist.

Further in the distance some of the red-furred canine aliens seemed to be operating vendor stalls—exchanging what looked like bundles of food with their seeming customers.

Yvette twitched her nose automatically, wishing to catch the smell in the air, but of course, all she smelled was the pristine, filtered air inside her spacesuit.

Yvette supposed that the group of crewmembers from *The Lucky Boomerang* must look odd, standing in front of their docked ship in their shimmery spacesuits and helmets. None of the aliens here seemed to be wearing spacesuits inside the station.

Wait, no, that wasn't quite true—Yvette spotted a creature with a complex helmet over its head. What she could see of its body was blue with long, trailing, silky-looking fins. It looked like a fish, and it even swam through the air. Yvette wondered how—did its helmet provide a small pocket of anti-gravity? The dollies being used to move cargo about hovered as well, and pockets of anti-gravity were how *The Lucky Boomerang* had found this station in the first place, so the mouse supposed it was possible. It still felt fantastical and unreal to see it happening in front of her with her own eyes. Though, the framing of her spacesuit helmet around her field of vision made it almost seem like yet another one of the video feeds that they'd all watched together back in engineering.

She wished the other mice were out here with her, seeing this too. With their own eyes, not filtered through the video feed each of their spacesuits was sending back to the ship, only a few feet behind them.

As odd as Yvette imagined that *The Lucky Boomerang* crewmembers looked in their shimmery, translucent spacesuits, none of the aliens had paid the slightest attention to them. They were all too busy with their own lives.

"Captain," Trugger's voice came over the radio in Yvette's helmet, and presumably the helmets of the others. "The air here is perfectly safe, according to the readings I'm getting. Permission for us to remove our helmets?"

Yvette was sure she imagined it, because Captain Kipper was so strong and brave, but she thought she heard a frightened crack in the tabby's voice as she said, "Permission granted."

Yvette eagerly unlatched the faceplate in her spacesuit's hood that served as a helmet and flipped it back over her head, letting her large round ears feel the whisper of different air sigh across her fur and the confusion of smells fill her twitching nose. Suddenly, the reality of her situation was something she could deny no longer: this was real; she could smell the cacophony of creatures and feel the air they shared moving through her whiskers.

Yvette was standing on (the shoulder of an otter on) an interstellar space station, filled with alien beings that she hadn't known inhabited this universe mere days ago. She wanted her friends to experience this too. She didn't want to keep this experience for just herself. She wanted to share. And she had an idea...

"Captain," Yvette squeaked. "The air smells so fresh and good." Complicated and delicious scents mixed with the profusion of creaturely smells indicating all the other life here. "So much fresher than aboard our ship. Wouldn't it be better to open the airlock up—" Yvette pointed with her tiny paw toward a nearby docking berth where a green, reptilian creature lounged in what looked like a lawn chair in front of an open airlock. "—like the other spaceships have done? We could air out the stale air we've been breathing and re-breathing all through the mission."

Silence greeted Yvette's suggestion. She looked at the captain and saw her green eyes were dilated, and her gray ears flattened, still inside the hood of her spacesuit, although she'd unlatched and removed the faceplate. She held the faceplate in her paws like a portable computer pad, and it would function that way, letting her communicate with Obsidian back on the ship. She looked overwhelmed. It must be frightening to face such a patina of the unknown while feeling wholly responsible for the lives of an entire crew and the results of such a bewildering first contact. And yet the captain pulled herself together, looked at the mouse on Trugger's shoulder, and smiled. "Yes, that does sound like a good idea."

Yvette sensed that the captain understood exactly what her plan had been getting at: letting the rest of the crew join them, even if only by lurking inside the opened airlock.

Trugger worked the controls, re-opening first the outer airlock door and then, overriding the ship's fail safes, also opening the inner one. Meanwhile, Captain Kipper radioed back to the crew onboard, explaining what was happening.

So, by the time the airlock was fully open, all of the engineers and even Sequoia, who had turned down the option of coming on this mission, were crowded around the opened inner door.

Yvette caught Josie's eye, and an electric spark of joy passed between them. Both mice grinned. Then Yvette jumped down from Trugger's shoulder, ran back partway into the airlock, and gestured for her three mice friends to come join her.

"Isn't this place amazing?" Yvette squeaked, and as she saw her friends' answering grins, for the first time, it really sank in that she was an interstellar traveler, surrounded by other interstellar travelers, a citizen of more than a country or world or even a whole solar system.

They might be tiny, but they were citizens of the galaxy.

And it was time to explore!

CHAPTER 27
AMELIA

As all the rest of the crew absorbed the chaotic view of alien lifeforms on this interstellar space station, Amelia only had eyes for the humans among the crowd. She wanted to rush toward the first one she saw—a human with pinkish skin and long black hair—and fall at the woman's feet. She wanted to forget everything about adulthood and civility and kiss the woman's boots, touching the fabric that clothed her, rubbing her tongue along a surface that touched a human's skin. She wanted to roll on her back and laugh and bark and beg the human to tell her she'd been a Good Dog.

It was the most confusing, silliest feeling Amelia had ever experienced, bubbling up through her, and leaving her light-headed. There were humans dotted throughout the crowd here, mixed in with the avians, insects, fish-like creatures, and all the orange-furred pointy-eared canine beings. Amelia's hackles raised at the sight of those strange alien dogs—they looked a little like Shelties or Collies with their bushy manes, but much, much taller. Taller than the humans. Jealousy burned the underside of Amelia's floppy ears: *why were these dogs here? Why had they been allowed to know humans their whole lives? Why did they walk among the First Race as if it meant nothing to them?*

Had humans left the dogs on Earth behind and *forgotten about them* because they'd found better dog friends in space?

Oh doggarned damnation, Amelia was thinking in blasphemies. Humans had not abandoned dogs. They had gone ahead, paving the way.

Maybe none of these humans had spared a glance for her, because they could sense Amelia's faith was so weak it would falter at the sight of them and the heaven they'd prepared for her to find. Maybe she truly was a Bad Dog.

"I'm not sure we should split up..." Captain Kipper said, finally pulling her spacesuit hood all the way down and seemingly replying to something Trugger had suggested. "This place is a lot bigger than Deep Sky Anchor."

"It's bigger than any otter space station," Trugger said.

Amelia tore her gaze away from a human with long black hair who was loading crates into the docking berth right next to *The Lucky Boomerang's* (*maybe Amelia could gain her favor and prove she was a Good Dog by helping load those crates for her?*) and turned to look at Captain Kipper's discussion with Trugger, who now had all four mice perched on his shoulders. Two mice on each side. Each mouse pointed a tiny paw toward some thrilling view in the distance, whiskers trembling with excitement on each of them. There were so many thrilling things to see that the mice's paws jabbed wildly at the air, pointing out one view after another.

Even the pair of dachshund brothers—the only other dogs on the ship—seemed delighted by the array of sights in front of them all.

Amelia didn't understand any of them. Her crewmates were standing near humans—actual members of the First Race, living GODS—and they were excited by the sight of a few giant insects or aliens with elephantine trunks? What did those things matter compared to living humans?

"I don't know, Kipper," Trugger said. "A little *reconnaissance*

—" He drew out the word in the silly, faux-pretentious way that he had. "—is always a good idea, right? And we'll cover more ground if we split up."

"You just want to play mount for those mice who've finally all settled on your shoulders at the same time," Kipper countered.

Trugger shrugged, causing the mice to giggle, partly with surprise at the rolling motion and partly with the giddiness of it all. "Maybe," he agreed. "But two birds fly farther when they fly in opposite directions."

"That... makes... no sense." Kipper frowned, then glanced, surprisingly at Amelia. "What do you think? As you pointed out, you've studied humans more than any of the rest of us, and according to Obsidian's translations, this is a human-run station."

Amelia had truly thought of herself as an expert on humans until mere minutes ago. But now, she was faced with the actuality of humans, and it made no sense to pretend that she knew anything at all. The First Race knew everything; Amelia was nothing but an acolyte, following footprints long left behind, trying to trace their path. A path that had led here. The humans were here. Anything Kipper wanted to know, she should ask the humans.

And yet, Amelia had a role to play in this crew, and she didn't know what to do other than play it through. Humans stood only twenty, forty, or fifty paces from her... and yet, they were still separated from her by an impossible gulf. They didn't look at her. They didn't notice her. And Amelia knew better— mostly—than to fall at their feet and roll about like a puppy on a sugar high.

"If this is a human-run station," Amelia said each word carefully, slowly, feeling her way. "Then I believe we're safe here." She gestured with a curly-furred paw. "Look how peaceful it is— all these aliens, going about their lives, organized by the holy power of…" Her voice broke off. She wanted to cry. There were humans who could have heard her words, the timbre of her voice, caught the sound of her speaking… if they were listening. And none of them were.

Why were none of her gods listening to her?

Didn't they care?

Didn't humans Love Good Dogs and Care about them? Weren't the First Race out here in space, specifically because they Loved and Cared about Good Dogs and wanted to prepare the perfect New Home for them?

If the Members of the First Race were ignoring her, did that mean Amelia wasn't a Good Dog?

Kipper didn't seem to care that Amelia had broken off mid-thought. The tabby cat captain, who stood only thigh-high to the humans mixed into the crowds on this station, was looking at those crowds very seriously. She nodded. "I think you're right."

Amelia noticed the differences in their words: Amelia had said she *believed*; Kipper said she *thought*.

Amelia didn't know what to think right now. But she did still believe. She believed. She believed so hard. She would not let go of that belief.

At least… She didn't think she would let go of that belief…

The thought entered her mind, small and unwanted, but undeniably there: maybe her belief wasn't as strong as it should be. Right now, her belief felt tenuous, like a waving curtain, shielding her from seeing a bigger truth hidden behind it. A horrible truth.

"Alright," Kipper said, waving a paw at Trugger and the eager mice on his shoulders. "Go do some reconnaissance. Don't get lost." She turned her feline gaze to the rest of the crew, crowded around the open airlock. "Who wants to go with them?"

Several paws raised—Georgie's, Katasha's, and Hedda's. The cats' eyes were wide with curiosity, and Georgie's floppy black ears were pricked up with interest, even though he couldn't hear anything with them. Freddy, Sequoia, and the bonded pair of Nioli and Gy'krr looked less certain; Nioli's tentacles had blanched to a pale shade of pink under the translucent covering of her spacesuit.

Kipper waved her paw at the three crewmembers with their paws eagerly raised and said, "Go on then, follow Trugger, and stick together." Then she turned to the remaining group and said, "Freddy and Sequoia, would you stay here and keep an eye on the situation at our airlock?"

The squirrel and dachshund exchanged a glance.

"You're not asking us to guard it?" Freddy asked, sounding uncertain. He was a small dog, like Amelia. Smaller than his brother Georgie. And Sequoia, being a squirrel, was even smaller than him. They wouldn't make very good guards in this crowd of giant red-furred canines and other large aliens. The only *Lucky Boomerang* crewmember who would make a good guard was Gy'kyrr with her sharp talons, her long, strong legs, and Nioli's powerful tentacles reaching over her shoulders like strange, grasping wings.

"No," Kipper said. "Just keep an eye out. You can always go inside and close the airlock behind you. Basically, play lookout for us. Lock up if there's any... uh... danger. And contact us over the suit radios; then let us in when we get back. I mean, hopefully, it won't come to that." Kipper looked around at the chaos —the peaceable chaos—surrounding them again. Then she turned back to the remaining crewmembers in the group who hadn't been assigned a role—Amelia, Gy'krr, and Nioli. "The four of us are going to see if we can find whoever's in charge of this station and... I don't know... forge some kind of first contact peace treaty?"

Nioli signed for both her and Gy'krr, "We would like to be part of that mission."

Amelia nodded, curtly. She couldn't bring herself to say more words, feeling the weight of all the humans around them. Not right now. But maybe soon. Maybe Captain Kipper would find the human in charge, and everything would fall into order. It would all make sense the way it was supposed to.

Kipper held up the spacesuit helmet faceplate, a simple squarish oval of clear plastic, in front of her like some kind of metaphorical shield and said, "You can hear me, right, Obsidian?" Text streamed over the glassy surface of the faceplate, and Kipper nodded, seemingly content with the octopus's reply. "Okay, great, that means we have half a chance of understanding what anyone else says to us." She looked up and glanced around the giant docking hangar, eyes glazed and ears held at half mast. She looked nearly as overwhelmed as Amelia felt. "If only we had a way for them to understand us..."

Nioli signed with her tentacles, which had turned a paler shade of soft violet: "With this many different species aboard a single station, we're clearly seeing representatives of many different worlds. They must have more experience breaking through language barriers than the small collection of species we represent from our solar system."

Kipper nodded again. Then she tilted her head, ears skewing unevenly, as she stared curiously at the bonded octopus-raptor pair. "Do you usually speak in sign language when bonded together?" she asked. "I'm sorry if that's an impertinent question... I'm just... Surprised. And I guess I haven't seen the two of you bonded much before. And this is all a lot—" She gestured at everything. "—and I suddenly wondered, and I need to get ahold of my tongue before I go talking to a bunch of complete aliens and blurting out something unforgivable, don't I?"

Nioi's violet tentacles wriggled in an octopus form of laughter, and Gy'krr's spade-like, feathered head bowed, seeming to try to hide a smile. When the two of them recovered from their amusement at Captain Kipper's discomfiture, Nioli signed, "Yes, we're more comfortable signing when we think together. It's part of why we've stayed together, even after the revolution liberating octopi—our octopus self is more dominant, which is very unusual. But it feels right to us. We like to be together. We like it when we speak with our tentacles. And we don't mind you asking."

Amelia frowned at all the words looping through the air in front of her in the shapes of those dancing tentacles. She'd clearly come a long way at reading sign language since joining the crew of *The Lucky Boomerang*, but it was still a struggle.

And nothing should have been a struggle here... not with humans so close at paw.

"Alright," Kipper said. "This is wildly stereotypical—straight out of the cheesiest of the old sci-fi B-movies preserved from the human era—but we need to find who's in charge. So, Obsidian, is there any chance that you can give me a sound clip that says something simple like 'Take me to your leader' in a language that someone here might understand?"

Amelia, Nioli, and Gy'krr all crowded around Kipper to watch the text that began scrolling over the faceplate when Obsidian answered. He answered in the affirmative, providing a short sound clip that Kipper could play by pressing a digital button on the faceplate screen. Alongside it, Obsidian offered sound clips that he said should mean approximately 'yes,' 'no,' and 'confusion.'

Drawing a deep breath, perking her ears as tall as they would stand, and squaring her shoulders, Kipper prepared herself. Amelia was awed by the bravery and audacity of this tabby cat who didn't even believe in the power, supremacy, and love of the First Race. For all Kipper knew, these humans could be totally indifferent to a ship of cats, dogs, mice, and other sundry animals from the world they'd fled many generations ago. It must be lonely to feel that way. And yet, Kipper charged off, straight toward the closest human.

Captain Kipper stood barely waist-high to the human woman

with the long dark hair, but she held the faceplate up and pressed a pawpad carefully to the screen. A strange series of sounds emitted from the faceplate, and the human's expression turned intense and concerned.

Amelia felt like she could have fainted. She half wished she actually would, because the stress of seeing one of her gods look at her crewmate with such confusion felt like an icicle to the heart. Surely, the confusion would pass. Surely, this would all begin to make sense.

But no, the human shrugged. An oddly familiar and understandable gesture considering the string of nonsense syllables she spoke following the shrug. It was a human's voice—soft and musical and a sound Amelia had waited her whole life to hear, and yet, the sounds meant nothing to her. Just gibberish.

Amelia wanted to press closer to Kipper and look at the screen to see how Obsidian translated the words—she was desperate to understand the words of her god. But her paws wouldn't move, wouldn't take her closer.

Kipper pressed the screen again; Amelia couldn't see whether it was to say 'yes,' 'no,' or 'confusion.' But the human spoke more gibberish and then pointed into the distance, across the crowd filling the docking hangar.

"If I've understood correctly," Kipper said, "there are administrative offices for the station that way. Let's go!" She sounded surprisingly chipper about the situation, even with all its uncertainty.

Amelia couldn't understand right now how anyone could feel anything short of absolute euphoria—being in the presence of humans!—or totally crushing despair. Those felt like the only two feelings left in the universe, and she could feel herself teetering toward the latter one. None of this was anything she could have expected. And none of it felt like the warm blanket of Safety and Acceptance and Approval and Complete Love that she had always known Humans would Provide.

Each step through the crowd made Amelia's paws feel heavier, and each glance she cast at a human in the crowd—only to see the human gaze right past her, usually over her head, totally indifferent to her presence and the Work she'd done all her life to be a Good Dog—made the poor dog's heart sink farther into her stomach. She felt like the roiling acid in her belly would dissolve her heart entirely, and there'd be nothing left of her to Love Humans Back, even if They Finally Did Shower Her With The Praises She'd Been Awaiting.

Amelia's paws stopped moving beneath her. She barely felt like she was still inside her body. She certainly didn't seem to be able to control it anymore.

A moment and a few strides later, Captain Kipper stopped and looked back at the stalled dog, quirking one ear into a questioning tilt. "Is something wrong?"

"I can't do this," Amelia replied. The words came from her mouth, but they didn't feel like they came from her heart. Her heart was screaming inside her, but acid in her stomach was roiling and her paws tingled with numbness. Her head felt like it would float away. Amelia was having a panic attack. She'd had them before, but never this bad.

Why now?

Why did she have to panic now?

Amelia wanted nothing more than to stride into the administrative offices of this space station, look into the eyes of the human in charge, and feel the world fall into order around her as she helped negotiate the future congress between the Good Dogs of Earth and the Holy Humans of Here.

But...

A creeping, hollowing, horrible fear filled her: that wasn't what would happen. Nothing would fall into place. The world was going to be out of order, everything discordant and confusing, and infinitely lonely for the rest of eternity.

Because the humans here didn't care that she'd come so far to see them.

They didn't care about her at all.

"What do you mean, 'you can't do this'?" Captain Kipper asked.

Amelia shook her head, staring at her paws. It was all she could manage. But then words found their way out of her mouth: "I need to go back to the ship."

Captain Kipper looked like she was about to ask 'why?' but then thought better of it. She shrugged and said, "You can help Sequoia and Freddy keep lookout."

Amelia nodded.

Then she turned herself around and walked away from her gods.

CHAPTER 28
KIPPER

Kipper watched Amelia walk away, back toward their spaceship. It shouldn't bother her to have the government dog who she'd never wanted on her ship leave her side. But it felt wrong.

Kipper was just one cat. A tabby who'd grown up in a cattery, poor and undereducated, without a real support system. She had her siblings, and she'd made friends over the years. But deep inside, she still felt like a lone cat who had to fight for herself.

She felt so entirely, completely unqualified to be here, representing an entire planet. Sure, she had Nioli and Gy'krr by her side, but they represented Jupiter. Not Earth. And sure, she could call Trugger back to her side. He would always come when she needed him. But he would support her—not take the weight off her shoulders.

The chain of choices Kipper had made in her life—searching for something better than oppression by First Racer dogs, fighting for the lives of the cats on New Persia when they were under attack, and refusing to let go of her ideals when President Truman tried to shut down her space program—had brought her inexorably here.

She was the only cat for this job.

Kipper turned herself back in the direction that the human had pointed her in and began walking, one paw in front of the other, making herself step closer and closer to whatever she would find in this space station's administrative offices.

Perhaps Kipper shouldn't have been surprised to find red tape—rooms with people in them who passed her along from one person to the next, some of them human and some more bizarre (one was clearly a robot, built from clanking metals), making her wait while they conferred with each other, trying to decide what to do with the waist-high cat in a spacesuit, backed up by a looming octopus-raptor being, speaking a language they didn't know and haphazardly trying to communicate via sound-snippets played on her translucent faceplate computer screen.

In all, it only took fifty minutes—though it felt like hours—for Kipper, Nioli, and Gy'krr to be passed along from person to person until they landed in a final room, sitting in front of a human with short-clipped, frizzy hair and light brown skin with a parrot sitting on either shoulder. One parrot was yellow and blue; the other red and green. And the way they sat on the human's shoulders made Kipper think of Trugger with all four mice riding him like a giant otter-shaped tram. It also made her think of depictions of pirates in ancient human movies.

Did everyone in space—otters and humans alike—think that deep down they were pirates?

The human spoke, forming a gibberish slew of syllables that ran together, a complete stew of sounds that Kipper couldn't make the slightest sense of. But she looked down at the translucent screen in her paws and saw words appear: *"Attempted translation: '...can translate... speak... practice... learn takes time...'"*

Kipper glared at the words and their broken nature. They weren't a lot to go on, but Obsidian's guesses about what the human was saying were certainly better than the gibberish slew of syllables itself.

Kipper drew a deep breath through her sharp teeth and said, "My translator says that you might be telling me to speak a lot of words so that you can practice understanding my language? Actually, I have no idea if that's what this translation means, but it's my best guess. So, I'm going to try saying a lot of words and hope that somehow it gives you the raw data that you need to get your translators working. Speaking of which..." Kipper glanced around the room, trying to spot a device that looked like it might be a translator or computer of some kind. "...what kind of device are you using for translation?"

The blue and yellow parrot flapped its wings; the red and green one said in a perfect copy of Kipper's stressed out voice and querulous intonation, "...what kind of device are you using for translation?"

Kipper blinked at the bird. "You're the translator," she said.

The blue one flapped its wings again. The red one repeated, "Translator."

Looking back down at the screen in her paws, Kipper saw a message from Obsidian reading, *I can't translate all of what you just said, but I think this audio clip should say, 'Speak a lot to teach translator?' Or hopefully, something close to that.*" Kipper pressed the button with a paw pad that started the screen playing the new audio clip. Then she looked carefully at the human and parrots for their reaction to the sounds.

The human raised her eyebrows, looking surprised and pleased. Kipper might not understand the human's language, but she'd seen enough old human movies to be able to do a rudimentary job of reading their facial expressions.

The blue parrot squawked, and the red one *laughed*. There was no other correct description of that sound.

Despite all the strange things that had happened to Kipper in her life, none of them had prepared her for visiting a human space station and having a parrot laugh at her.

And it wasn't like it was an alien parrot. No, Kipper was

dead sure that these parrots were Earth parrots, uplifted like she had been.

For a moment, she felt a flash of anger: why were the parrots here? Why had humans brought parrots into space and left cats, dogs, otters, and her *behind*. Kipper had had to fight her way into space, pushing back against religious dogs who would be furious to find out about these parrots, but the parrots? They'd been up here on a human space station, living side by side with humans all along.

Kipper's whole life, even when her paws had never left the solid foundation of Earth, these parrots had been living in the sky, light-years away, in a completely different part of the galaxy, circling a completely different pair of suns.

Why were parrots better than her? Why were they more worth bringing along on a journey into the marvels of the extended universe?

Was it because they could translate?

Since cats had to be given human speech through uplift, rather than being able to mimic it in their own right, they weren't worth as much?

Kipper wasn't a religious cat, but she suddenly understood why Amelia hadn't been able to handle all of this; why the deeply devout dog had needed to return to their spaceship in the face of this all.

This was going to be a hard transition for all the uplifted animals of Earth, not just the religious First Racer ones. Humans had raised them up, been their parents, and then abandoned them. Returning to Earth with news of what those abandoning parents had been up to for all these generations was going to cause a lot of emotions. Kipper could hardly even imagine what effects it would have on Uplifted States society, let alone the interconnected web of societies that made up the entire solar system.

But this was the way forward, and you don't stop going

forward just because it's scary.

So, Kipper turned to her crewmates—Nioli and Gy'krr—and after indicating the hulking feathered raptor and twisty tentacles of the octopus with a gesture of her paw, she introduced them to the human and parrots. She briefly described the different societies filling the solar system—the raptors and octopi of Jupiter; the otters living in the spaces between worlds; and the cats, dogs, mice, and squirrels on Earth. She talked about the other members of her crew—the ones back on the ship and the ones exploring this space station. She used a lot of words, and she watched the two parrots tilt their heads inquisitively, focusing on every word she said, even if they couldn't possibly be understanding them all yet.

As Kipper spoke, the parrots took turns muttering quietly into the human's ears, possibly translating, possibly discussing something entirely unrelated. Kipper had no way to know.

When she ran out of words, Kipper glanced down at the screen in her paws and saw a message from Obsidian: *"You know I can't possibly translate all that."*

Kipper laughed in spite of herself at the image of Obsidian, back aboard *The Lucky Boomerang* twisting his tentacles into a tangle trying to keep up with all the words she was saying and ideas she was trying to convey.

When Kipper looked back up at the parrots and human watching her, the human said a few gibberish syllables. The blue parrot repeated them, but this time they actually made sense: "And your name?"

"My name?" Kipper asked, surprised. Then she realized, in all the words she'd said and introductions she'd made—including those to crewmembers who weren't here—she'd forgotten to introduce herself. "I'm Kipper Brighton," she said. "Captain of *The Lucky Boomerang*. And I'm here to forge a connection between the peoples in my solar system and—" Words failed her; she simply gestured with her paw in a way that included everything around them. The room they were in. The space station it was part of. The aliens walking through that space station. And all their space ships docked along its spinning rings.

All the stars in the sky.

All the space in between.

Everything.

Kipper was here to forge peace between her world and everything else in the universe.

It was a lot of responsibility for one small tabby cat. But she knew her friends back home would have her back—Emily who'd ascended to become some kind of grand high octopus leader; Jenny running the Europa Base; Captain Cod with the fastest ship in the solar system, short of her own *Lucky Boomerang*; and her siblings—both blood and found—Petra, Alistair, and Trudith with whatever political power they could still manage on Earth.

Kipper might feel lonely carrying this responsibility on her shoulders, but she wasn't really alone.

EPILOGUE

he Lucky Boomerang stayed docked at the interstellar space station for more than a month before it was time to head home to Earth, bearing a treasure trove of new knowledge, strange goods, and even one of the translator parrots who wanted to come along.

Trugger and the mice had become regular customers at several of the food carts during their month-long visit, and Kipper learned about interstellar law. Most importantly, she learned that the humans running the space station—Crossroads Space Station—wouldn't trade or deal with societies that didn't afford equal rights to all their members. This meant, if dogs wanted to oppress cats and ban them from traveling to space, then these humans wouldn't want to have anything to do with them.

Cats would be as free as dogs, if the dogs wanted humans to acknowledge them.

Kipper didn't think that any other single fact had ever made her feel more vindicated in her entire life.

Communication between the crewmembers of *The Lucky Boomerang* and the many peoples of Crossroads Station had gotten easier when Obsidian uncovered an archive of ancient human movies on the space station's computer systems, some of which overlapped with the ancient human movies that dog and cat archeologists had managed to recover over the years. And most importantly, the versions on the Crossroads Station database had subtitles, translating the old human languages (which cats and dogs already knew how to translate) into Solanese, the most commonly spoken language on the space station.

So, between the translation programs Obsidian was able to write and the parrots who chose to keep hanging out with the interesting new spaceship that had docked at their station, communication went from halting and uncertain to something that flowed as easily as a frisbee flying through the sky.

Or a boomerang.

But as much as Kipper reveled in the discoveries they were making—and Trugger and the mice seemed to want to live on Crossroads Station forever—they needed to take everything that they'd learned back home. She needed to return her crew to their families.

Kipper spoke with each member of her crew individually, feeling them out, before she declared it was time to go. And when it came down to it, the only crewmembers who wanted to stay behind were Nioli and Gy'krr. The bonded octopus-raptor pair had no place back in the solar system where they felt comfortable or needed, but here? They could be liaisons between two worlds—the complicated interstellar hub of Crossroads Station and their own relatively small, simple solar system.

Many of the dogs—President Truman, especially—back home would be furious with Kipper for leaving an octopus and raptor behind as their solar system's representative diplomats. But those dogs could go to hell—their own personal hell of realizing that the humans out here were just people, living their own lives, and didn't imbue a bunch of canines hundreds of lightyears away with an inalienable right to oppress the other animals around them.

Everyone else, when push came to shove, wanted to go home, even if some of them were more ready for it than others.

Amelia had spent many hours crying over the shattering of her religious beliefs. But Kipper had arranged for one of the humans who'd been teaching her about interstellar law—a kind one who didn't entirely understand what had been explained to her about the dogs on Earth but who wanted to help—to come to *The Lucky Boomerang* and speak with Amelia for awhile.

Amelia had listened to the human talk about her life on Crossroads Station—the day to day minutia of being a human living a normal life for a human—and then the human, generously, had listened to Amelia's own halting, sob-wracked words, as she processed the profound disappointment of her deity being no more godly than any other mundane person. The dog's tears had dried up. She had found a way to cope with learning that her gods... were only human.

The human had even given Amelia a hug before leaving. The curly-furred dog had closed her brown eyes as tight as she could and absorbed all the warmth and love that she could find in that embrace. A human's arms, wrapped around her body! A human! And her! And then... the moment was over. And Amelia resolved to move on.

Neither Sequoia nor Amelia planned to stay with *The Lucky Boomerang* after returning to Earth. The squirrel had been disappointed by the stars, nearly as badly as the dog had been disappointed by humans. They planned to go, together, back to Sequoia's family home in Europe and find their bearings anew.

Sequoia hadn't found what she'd been looking for in the stars—up close they weren't as she had imagined them, weren't friends waiting for her with their transcendent glow, weren't acorns she could collect, weren't deities anymore than humans were—but she'd found something else among them, something she might love even more. A funny, serious, kind of lost, curly-furred dog with a heart that burned like a star. A Good Dog, whether any humans ever said so or not.

And Yvette? She didn't care about winning first place in any contests any more. She was surrounded by friends and work she loved, and an entire universe of possibilities. She planned to stay a crewmember of *The Lucky Boomerang* for a long time, and she hoped that would involve visiting Crossroads Station again soon.

ABOUT THE AUTHOR

Mary E. Lowd is a prolific science-fiction and furry writer in Oregon. She's had more than 200 short stories and a dozen novels published, always with more on the way. Her work has won three Ursa Major Awards, ten Leo Literary Awards, and four Cóyotl Awards. She edited FurPlanet's ROAR anthology series for five years, and she is now the editor and founder of the furry e-zine *Zooscape*. She lives in a crashed spaceship, disguised as a house and hidden behind a rose garden, with an extensive menagerie of animals, some real and some imaginary.

For more information:
marylowd.com

To read Mary's short stories:
deepskyanchor.com

ALSO BY MARY E. LOWD

Otters In Space

Otters In Space

Otters In Space 2: Jupiter, Deadly

Otters In Space 3: Octopus Ascending

Otters In Space 4: First Moustronaut

Otters In Space Spinoffs

In a Dog's World

When A Cat Loves A Dog

Jove Deadly's Lunar Detective Agency (with Garrett Marco)

The Entangled Universe

Entanglement Bound

The Entropy Fountain

Starwhal in Flight

Entangled Universe Spinoffs

You're Cordially Invited to Crossroads Station

Welcome to Wespirtech

Beyond Wespirtech

Brunch at the All Alien Cafe

Xeno-Spectre

Hell Moon

The Ancient Egg

The Celestial Fragments (A Labyrinth of Souls Trilogy)

The Snake's Song

The Bee's Waltz

The Otter's Wings

Tri-Galactic Trek

Nexus Nine

Commander Annie and Other Adventures

The Necromouser and Other Magical Cats

The Opposite of Memory

Queen Hazel and Beloved Beverly

Some Words Burn Brightly: An Illuminated Collection of Poetry

Furry Fiction Is Everywhere (with Ian Madison Keller)